The Case of the Swan in the Fog
A 'Before Watson' Novel
(Book Three)

Further Reminiscenses of P.S.T.
(Based upon notes, newspaper clippings and
correspondence received from Sherlock Holmes)

By A. S. Croyle

Paperback ISBN 978-1-78705-224-6
ePub ISBN 978-1-78705-225-3
PDF ISBN 978-1-78705-226-0

Published in the UK by MX Publishing
335 Princess Park Manor, Royal Drive,
London, N11 3GX
www.mxpublishing.co.uk
Cover design by Brian Belanger

Big Barges full of yellow hay
Are moored against the shadowy wharf,
And, like a yellow silken scarf,
The thick fog hangs along the quay
        -Oscar Wilde – Symphony in Yellow

To Tim James, a friend, first reader, fan and a fighter.

PROLOGUE

June 8, 1944

The fog of war is lifting and hope, a feather perched in my soul, rises from its darkened chamber.

I thought of Sherlock Holmes, who would have rejoiced at the news, and it brought tears to my eyes. I wish he were here with me, listening to the good tidings on the BBC.

We have just learned that in early June, the United States and Great Britain assembled the largest number of soldiers and the greatest amount of equipment ever to launch and sustain an amphibious attack. Hour by hour, we hear accounts of the acts of heroism on the beaches of Normandy where the Allied forces invaded occupied Western Europe.

I had to smile when my dear brother, Dr. Michael Stamford—the man who introduced Sherlock Holmes to Dr. John Watson—rushed into my room, nearly losing his footing. Leaning on his cane, his voice quivering, he said, "Poppy, look at this!" as he handed me the financial edition with its front-page headline: *Tone Commendably Calm on War News.* Was a more British headline ever written?

I scanned the article quickly. The article began by stating, "The Stock Exchange took the news of the long-expected invasion of the Continent with commendable calmness." I could not help but be amused by the use of such phrases as "fairly busy," "inclined to dry up" and "understandably quiet" in front page reporting. The stories in other papers were a bit more dramatic. One article stated that "June 7th dawns with the allies securely in control of all five beach heads."Another report in *The Evening Standard* said that Churchill announced the successful massed air landings behind enemy lines."That story went on to describe the landing of four thousand ships and eleven thousand aircraft—"flying fortresses" bombing the beach.

Soon my grandson will be coming home. We received word that he was wounded, and we do not know the extent of his injuries, but I am hopeful, that, like Sherlock Holmes' faithful companion John Watson, the damage, both physical and emotional, will not be too great for him to resume the practice of medicine.

As I look out my bedroom window, however, I see another fog rolling in . . . and it is a reminder of days gone by, of the fogs that covered my beloved London in the past, smothering it and granting camouflage for criminals. Even my dear friend Oscar Wilde wrote about the awful, moving beast that shut out the sun in our fair city.

The fog never stopped Sherlock Holmes. He could unearth any clue and bring light to darkness. He entered the world to purge evil from London, to pounce on the beasts of the city's underbelly with his fresh ideas, his unorthodox methods, and a gentle, wordless expectation that his opinions would be taken as gospel. He moved through the world alone, trying to snuff out the grim and imaginative cruelties that man visits upon man. But he did let me in for just a little while. For a short time, we entered an unwritten sacrosanct contract, with Sherlock as Don Quixote and me as his Sancho. Then again, Sherlock tilted no windmills. He was born to slay dragons.

Sherlock Holmes kept secrets, even from Dr. Watson, his friend and biographer. Secrets about his friendship with my brother Michael who introduced Watson to Sherlock, secrets about himself, and definitely secrets about me and my involvement in many of his early cases. I am quite certain Dr. Watson never knew about the time Sherlock and I spent together in the Broads or that we designed a little sailing vessel, a replica of which Sherlock left me under the terms of his Last Will and Testament. I am sure Dr. Watson never knew about our affection for one another or about my long struggle to shed the heavy weight of my love for him. These were secrets Sherlock took to his grave.

I finally summoned the courage to part ways with Sherlock, to go on without him in my life, only because I had no choice. Ultimately, the relationship was unsustainable. I walked away from him over sixty years ago because I discovered it was easier to bury my feelings than to carry them around like a stone on my back. I struggled for years to carve out a new life far away from him, and the burden diminished; its consistency gradually went from a mantle of marble to a warm blanket to a gauzy veil.

But I kept up with his adventures. I read Dr. Watson's accounts of how Sherlock continued to try to transform London into a magic city of permanent peace.

But, oh, had he succeeded, how very bored he would have been.

For the first time since I learned of the bombing of Pearl Harbour, I am optimistic enough to set pen to paper as I turn my thoughts again to Sherlock. I shall set aside my fears and once again pause to reflect upon the happier—albeit frustrating and confusing—times of my youth when Sherlock and I meandered the streets of his beloved London, long before the bombs and shelters, before the breaking glass and shattered lives. I shall let my mind move through itself, looping back to those burnished memories, to those reflections and dreams that I had tried to tuck away. I shall re-create that short-lived, long-ago idyll that we shared when I tossed away reason and gave way to emotions.

I remain to this day somewhat overwhelmed with the pain of loss, for I never quite recognized myself after we parted, and I could never quite reconcile 'Before Sherlock' with 'After Sherlock.' The pendulum would swing back and forth. Even after all these years, even as I approach the age of ninety and the end of my life, I am as perplexed as ever about the rejection—his of me and mine of him.

But everything between still sparkles

.

Christmas Day 1879 was attended with nocturnal darkness in London. My parents would later tell me that even in the Broads of Norfolk from which I hail, the fog was remarkably thick throughout the day there as well.

I should have liked to share the festivities with my parents at our home, Burleigh Manor. My Aunt Susan, her ward, little Billy—the baby brother of one of Sherlock's homeless messengers—and my nephew, Alistair Alexander were there. I longed to be there to watch Alexander open gifts and to gaze at his joyful countenance; he so resembled his mother, my brother's late wife, my best friend Effie.

As doctors, we were needed in London. My brother Michael and my uncle, Dr. Ormond Sacker, both physicians at St. Bart's, had decided to forego the holiday celebration in the Broads, as had I. A great fog had snaked into London, covering her with a thick and ominous blanket, the blackest fog I ever saw. It was causing hundreds of people to become deathly ill. That very Christmas morning, Uncle had been summoned to treat the seventy-eight-year-old mother of the First Earl of Kimberly, John Wodehouse. Though she bore her illness with great fortitude, Uncle feared the worst. Disease and injuries caused by the fog had fairly devastated the city.

Sherlock had sent one of his homeless boys, whom he used as messengers and who helped him gather information, with a note in which he requested that I meet him "immediately at Bart's." Certain that my medical office was empty as it usually was, and worried that Sherlock

1

might be ill, I made my way from Regent's Park, where I resided with Uncle Ormond and Aunt Susan, to St. Paul's. The entire time my face was masked in a thick wool scarf.

I stopped for a few moments to pray, and then continued on my way, crossing Newgate into Giltspur Street until I reached St. Bart's Hospital.

I stopped to chat with Michael in the hallway but just for a moment. "Is he ill?" I asked.

"No, he's in the lab. Must be off, darling," Michael said.

"He" was Sherlock Holmes.

A bit miffed at the summons, I made my way to the lab. Sherlock was looking out the window. He did not turn around when I entered. As I removed my hat, scarf, cape and gloves, he said, "It's like a brown mass, isn't it, Stamford? Rising and hanging like a still, thick curtain between the world and the sky. It blots out the sun and the moon. I suppose this is rather propitious to amatory encounters. I'm told that the nymphs of the *pave* do unusually good business in this weather. Even I could be bold, perforce leave off my work and for a shilling or two accost a petticoat. If I were so inclined," he added.

I felt myself blush.

"Of course, for my young friend Archie, it's rather a good atmosphere for grave robbing as well," he continued.

The 'Archie' to whom he referred was Archibald William Wiggins, the oldest of the homeless boys who ran errands for Sherlock, but he was known on the streets as Bill Wiggins. His little brother Billy now resided, off and on, with my Uncle Ormond and Aunt Susan because the boys' mother was unreliable, but Wiggins refused to completely relinquish his place in Billy's life. Sherlock often said he hoped to turn little Billy into a proper page one day.

"This dense fog chokes our fair city, Stamford," Sherlock sighed. "The blacks cover and obscure everything from view. Very bad for the bees, you know. The damnable flying particles of soot settle everywhere. London stinks of the coal age.

"I would wager the casualty department here is filled with victims today. Omnibus and cab accidents," he said, still staring out the window. "I heard someone say that a man driving a horse and gig toward town ran up against a granite wall and was thrown with great force upon the footpath. Another man ran into a shop window on St. James and broke upward of forty squares of glass. The other night, some drunkards ended up falling into the Thames and drowned. I am surprised we have not heard of another collision on the river, like the one at Vauxhall Bridge or the *Princess Alice* sinking."

I cringed, remembering the terrible collision on the Thames River the previous year when the *Princess Alice*, a paddle-boat steamer, was cut in half by a large cargo ship.

"But London is never swathed in ordinary darkness, is she?" he added as he turned around. Seeing me, he exclaimed, "Poppy! What are you doing here?"

"You sent for me, Sherlock."

"Where did your brother go? I was just speaking to him."

"He left several minutes ago, Sherlock. It is I who heard your soliloquy."

"Michael left?" he asked, a puzzled expression on his face. "I did not notice."

Of course, he didn't. Sherlock often went into a world of his own, delving so deeply into his brain attic that he did not realize the person to whom he had been speaking had left the room. This eccentricity had increased of late. He was getting more cases, solving each crime with breathtaking rapidity, and he had so suppressed his emotions that whatever remnants of them that were left were deeply tucked away and rarely revealed.

"Pea soup. The entire city is like pea soup. Brown and greenish and smoky and so dark that vehicles over in Piccadilly keep running into each other," he mumbled, as he walked over to the counter and settled behind his microscope.

"I must ask you about Wiggins, Sherlock. You mentioned grave-robbing. Please do not tell me that he has become involved in some grave-robbing scheme."

He arched an eyebrow. "I am not his keeper, Poppy. Nor are you."

I heaved a sigh and wandered over to a corner of the room where I saw a box full of things I did not recognize. "What is all this, Sherlock? More bee paraphernalia?"

"Yes, more bee equipment. I must keep the swarm safe." He fixed his eyes on the slide beneath the microscope.

4

I bent over the container and perused its contents. There was a collection of everything from hive stands to Honey Supers, bee brushes to pry bars to separate boxes from frames, and veil and gloves.

"Do be careful," he warned, not looking up. "The equipment is quite dear for a man on my fluctuating income, and I had a devil of a time finding the proper bottom board to ventilate the new hive."

I turned to look at him. He was now almost twenty-six; his birthday was just days away, on 6 January.

He was just twenty, two years my senior, when we met in the spring of 1874. He had not changed much, externally or internally. Even then, he was a lone wolf, determined to seek his own path; headstrong and unconventional in his thinking. Determined to harness the powers of science and logic and deduction and his own incredible intellect, he made it his life's mission to peel back the truth, to dispel myths and to solve mysteries. He approached each new case as if it were his first—or his last, with the enthusiasm of an inventor about to reveal his latest innovation. I worried about his zeal, his lack of discretion, his lack of appreciation for the dangers he often faced in our crime-ridden city. Sometimes in pursuit of a criminal, he was like a young boy swimming in the sea, unaware of the downward spiral, the violent churning of a tidal sinkhole and the swells that could drag him into the depths of the ocean. Where danger was concerned, he could engage in uncustomary impetuousness. Whether he admitted it or not, Sherlock sought the immortality of fame.

His hair was dark, his eyes were grey and piercing beneath heavy, tufted brows. He was very tall and gaunt, quick and supple. His face was eager with a long beak-like nose. His fingers were long and thin; I loved to watch them plucking away at his violin, the sounds from which often reminded me of his strident voice. As was generally the case, today he wore a tweed suit. But I liked to envision him wandering around his room at Oxford in his purple dressing gown; he seemed so much more human and so much less a calculating machine when dressed thus. I remember he'd had a litter of pipes on his mantel there, but he most often smoked an oily, clay pipe when he was lost in thought, or his Cherrywood pipe on the occasions that he was inclined toward dispute and argument. I noticed his briarwood pipe near the microscope today. I had not yet determined its consanguinity to Sherlock's temperament. As strange and indifferent to human nature as he often seemed to be, to me Sherlock was, as the poet Yeats described someone he greatly admired, "the most human person alive," but the hardest to understand.

"I must take great care with the bees in this abominable weather," he muttered. "They must be wrapped. Dr. Haviland tells me that roofing paper does the trick." He looked up, his eyes vacant. "Oh, and that reminds me. I need to take a sample of propolis to examine it."

"Propolis?"

"Bee glue. It is a resinous mixture that honey bees collect from tree buds, sap flows, and other botanical sources." He returned his gaze to the slide and said, "There's something for you in the container, Poppy."

"For me? Something to do with bees?"

"No, nothing to do with bees. Have a look. I bought it from Morse Hudson at his art shop on Kennington Road. His mother wrapped it for me."

"Mrs. Hudson? Victor's former housekeeper?"

"Yes, Mrs. Hudson. Who else would be Morse's mother?"

I bent over the container again, carefully shifted some of the contents and found a small box. It was gaily wrapped in coloured paper that was marbled. My mother often used this technique for wrapping gifts, but she preferred to present gifts in keepsake boxes crafted from paper maché, decorated with paints and trinkets. My Aunt Susan usually crafted cloth gift bags in which small gifts could be hung from trees.

Sherlock's gesture surprised me . . . not just that Sherlock was actually presenting me with a Christmas gift but that it was not wrapped in something practical like brown paper or a newspaper with an article he wished me to read.

"What is it?"

"Well, you shall know when you open it."

I quickly unwrapped the gift. Inside was a small velvet box which contained a locket. "Sherlock, it's . . . it's beautiful."

"I thought you might place a photograph in it. You like that sort of thing, don't you?"

"I do! You know I do! You bought this at an art shop?"

"Morse says it is an antique."

7

"Sherlock, thank you ever so much," I said, rushing over to him. I touched his cheek and brushed my lips against his. He leaned back and away but our eyes held. For a moment, for just a fraction of a second, I saw in them what had flickered in the candlelight long ago in a cottage in Holme-Next-the-Sea during our one and only romantic interlude. It was but a brief flash of emotion, a spark that could give me a glimmer of hope if I allowed it to do so. I quickly suppressed my emotions. While Sherlock honed the science of deduction, I had forced myself to quash my feelings for him in self-defence.

My feet aching, I sat down across from him and removed my boots. "What do you have there?" I asked.

"We have here a dollop of blood from a mutilated swan," he said.

"A swan? Another swan like the one you examined for Mycroft after the Lord Mayor's Show last year?"

"Yes, and like the one we found after this year's show in November. Now this one has turned up. Just a month has passed, not a whole year. It seems we may have a serial killer of swans on the loose and his rage is escalating. It is quite baffling."

Serial killer . . . a term he had applied to the British Museum murders we'd solved the year before. "So, it's a series of murders like those we solved last year then? Only swans this time. Not people."

"Yes, precisely. And according to my brother Mycroft, if I do not solve this case forthwith, if I do not find out who is mutilating the Queen's swans, England shall fall."

2

I glanced at my watch, slipped my boots back on, and rose. I needed to get to my office.

"So I have no theory as yet," he said. "No working theory as to why someone would wish to harm Her Majesty's swans." Still staring at the slide, he said, "I have no facts from which to draw any conclusions except that which is before me . . . a sample of blood and the mutilated creature itself."

"And why did you decide to examine a blood sample?"

He sighed. "Mycroft insisted this time. Her Majesty wants to know if there is any possibility at all that whoever slaughtered the swan, while exhibiting disdain, even hatred for the Queen or the British government, may have had some degree of empathy for the creature."

"Empathy? But it's mutilated."

"Quite. But perhaps that was done after the fact— after the swan was killed, and the mutilation is only to send a message."

"Sherlock, I don't understand."

"There was a note, just as before."

He had mentioned the notes but had not shared their contents. His interest now had piqued and he was clearly ready to draw me into his investigation.

"Each time a swan is killed, a note is left which says, 'I showed it more mercy than was shown to me.' So," Sherlock continued, "it is Her Majesty's fervent hope that the killer did not want the swans to suffer unduly before the savagery. She is apparently quite fond of them."

"This is dreadful. Are you testing it for some poisonous concoction that would bring death on rapidly then? Like the poison used in the mercy killings last year?"

"Something similar to hydrocyanic acid, yes. I made a list of potential agents. Strychnine, for example, would . . . ."

". . . Not be commensurate with any sympathy for the creature," I interjected. "It has been tested on frogs because of their extreme sensibility to the effects, and when immersed in the poison, frogs are seized with violent tetanic convulsions, in which . . . ."

". . . In which," he interrupted, "the extremities become extended and the entire body becomes rigid. Yes, I know. I've experimented on frogs fresh from the pond. I observed that agitation hastens the action of even small quantities of the poison and a violent paroxysm can be induced by a sudden noise, like clapping."

"They would succumb quickly to the poison," I told him. "Swans, serene though they may look, can be quite violent, especially when someone intrudes upon their territory. They can be very aggressive in defence of their nests. I've heard them. They hiss, they whistle and snort, even the cygnets chirp and squawk harshly if they are disturbed. Mute swans often attack people who invade their territory, so the poison would act quickly, yes, but the death would hardly be merciful. And only someone familiar to the swans could get close enough at any rate."

Again, he lifted an eyebrow. "You know something of swans then, Poppy?"

"Of course. It is not just Her Majesty, the Dyers and the Vintners who lay claim to them."

"The who?"

"The city companies, the greatest subject swan owners on the river. They go annually to the Thames to mark the swans. But there are other owners throughout England. Did you never notice the swans in the river near Victor's house when we spent so much time there that summer?"

"I wasn't paying particular attention to the swans."

I pondered this statement momentarily. I wondered if he were trying to tell me that his focus had been on me that summer in the Broads when he'd visited Victor Trevor, Sherlock's one friend at Oxford and the man who had intended to marry me . . . the man who had left for his family's tea plantation in India when he discovered that Sherlock and I had feelings for each other. Or had Sherlock been focused on the little sailing vessel we designed when we spent many lazy days on the river bank during his visit?

"In fact, until Mycroft enlisted me in this enterprise," he said, "I thought of them as nothing more than something upon which to feast. We often had roast swan at Christmas. Our cook prepared it with several pounds of beef that were beaten into a fine mortar and stuffed inside the swan with some gourmand's onion, a stiff meal-paste laid upon the breast and served with strong beef gravy."

He smiled as if he'd just had a pleasant childhood memory. I'd come to know that there were few of those in that intrepid brain attic of his.

11

"In fact, despite the Queen's affection for the creatures," he went on, "she allowed her youngest son, Prince Leopold, to send a swan to Dr. Ackland, his tutor at Oxford for Christmas dinner. Do you remember Dr. Ackland?"

"Of course."

I had attended a rowing race with Victor at Oxford during Eights Week; my bull terrier bit Sherlock and he fell and sprained his ankle. That was how we met. Ackland was the physician who had treated Sherlock that day.

"There's a lovely old fable that a swan's life fades away in music," I said.

"Oh, Poppy. Like the legend of Apollo's bird singing his own requiem, I suppose. Such legends are as old as Homer's epics."

"And alluded to by Aristophanes and other ancient poets."

"You know that I have no use for poetry. Or poets," he added, and I knew instantly he was referring to my friend Oscar Wilde.

"In Shakespeare," I pressed on, "when King Henry is told that his father sang in the frenzy of death, he says, 'I am the cygnet to this pale, faint swan who chants a doleful hymn to his own death. And from the organ-pipe of frailty sings his soul and body to a lasting rest.' So Shakespeare may have believed—"

"Shakespeare! Cease!" he cried, laughing. "Perhaps poets and playwrights are unwilling to surrender to the fallacy of this belief, but nature, truth and science must prevail. "

Realizing that poetry and legends meant nothing to Sherlock, I asked, "Where is the swan?"

"Over there on the table beneath the sheet."

With a sigh, I went over to examine the swan's mandible. Lifting the sheet, I saw the royal marks. "There are marks. Were there marks on all of the swans' mandibles?"

He nodded. "I did notice marks, yes," he said.

"The marks are important, Sherlock. They display ownership."

"It hadn't occurred to me that this was how Mycroft knew it was a royal swan. They are all the same to me. Although now that I come to think of it, Mycroft did point out the marks. He mentioned the swan-mark of Eton. He said that it has an armed point and the feathered end of an arrow. He said this is represented by the nail-heads on the door of one of the inner rooms of the college."

"And you did not make note of that?"

"You know that I attended Harrow—rather because my father insisted on Eton and my brothers went there. So at the mention of Eton, my mind retreats. So then," he continued, "the royal swans are marked as well?"

"That's the purpose of the swan-upping. Swan-upping is an old, old tradition, Sherlock. It dates back to the twelfth century, I think. And the mute swan was given royal status centuries ago. I think the royal office of Keeper of the Swans dates back to the fourteenth century. Owning swans has long been a status symbol, Sherlock. Anyone stealing eggs or driving swans away at breeding time or slaughtering them is subject to a severe fine. And anyone

13

who is not a swanherd who carries a swan hook by which swans could be taken from the river is liable to a fine . . . something like thirteen shillings and sixty-some pence."

"You *do* know something about these creatures then."

"Certainly I do."

"How do you know all of this?" he asked.

"Because I am brilliant," I quipped. "Sherlock, seriously, we have a whole game of swans bearing our manorial mark at Burleigh Manor, and there are still many owners of swans in Norfolk and Suffolk. These marks—annulets, chevrons, crosses and crescents and such-like—are cut upon the bill with a knife. During the swan-upping, the cygnets, the babies, are given the same marks as their parents. The swans are driven into the bank where a cob and pen have their beaks examined for ownership and the babies are marked with the nicks. It's a very big festival."

"Wait, a cob and pen?"

"Cobs are the male swans. Pens are the females. The royal swan-mark remained unchanged from the commencement of the reign of King George III . . . three horizontal marks and two vertical on either side." I took up a pen and the notebook next to his microscope and drew the mark. "But the royal swan mark of Queen Victoria consists of five open pointed ovals, two cut lengthways and three cut transversely. Like this," I said, sketching out her mark. "Two nicks is the mark of the Vintners Company."

"Well, whatever is damaged on the creatures," he said, "the mandible remains intact. Even this recent one, which was horribly marred and disfigured . . . its mandible was not defaced."

"I believe this is significant, Sherlock. The act of mutilation is not intended as an act of rage against the swans. By choosing specifically royal swans, it is a message of what the killer would like to do to Her Majesty. Just like the last murder case we solved, the killer is sending a message."

3

"Let's get something to eat, Poppy," Sherlock said, standing and donning his waistcoat.

"You're going to eat while you are working?"

"This case is a puzzlement, I'll admit, but it certainly does not require intense intellectual activity."

"I really should go, Sherlock. You've seen what it's like out there. People are very ill."

As he shoved his right arm into the sleeve of his coat, he nodded. "Yes, I've been studying that aspect of this damn fog as well. I went to the Botanic Gardens in Regent's Park this morning and measured the barometer. It was unusually high, 30.54 at nine o'clock. A London fog is a complex phenomenon, isn't it? So different from its country counterparts. I remember from when we stayed at Holme-Next-the-Sea that a country fog can be somewhat pleasant."

I flinched momentarily, recalling the fog that swirled through the little village, but mostly remembering our night together there.

"Just a puff of white without smell and not all that disagreeable," Sherlock added. "It does not thicken after sunrise. It is pure, condensed vapour. But this with which we are faced here in the city is more than wind, temperature and vapour. It increases after the sun rises. A white handkerchief like the one you always carry attracts particles of soot like a magnet. It is a black haze that covers criminal activities, a perfect cover for intractable evil."

"*And* it endangers the health of our citizens," I said.

"Yes, yes. It does do damage to health and property because of the smoke and soot in the air. Winter is the worst, isn't it? On this holiday everyone is celebrating today—the coal being pushed out of private houses—*that* is what is primarily responsible for this blanket of darkness.

"Do you realize, Poppy, more than a million chimneys are breathing out smoke and soot and sulphurous acid and carbonic acid gas like fire from a dragon? We are in a crater filled with fumes.

"At least," he prattled on, "when there is some modicum of a breeze, the smoke removes itself to other parts of the atmosphere and no dark fog forms. But when the earth is not sufficiently warmed by the sun during our winter months, and the air near its surface cannot rise, the lowest atmospheric strata gain little heat and the conditions are perfect to produce such a fog. One filled with flakes of soot, particles of carbon . . . and these cannot evaporate."

"It's so sad, really," I said. "On a hot, breezy summer Sunday when the factories are not in operation, and fires not so much used for cooking, you can actually see the spires of St. Paul's or Albert Hall. Now it's all blurred with smoke."

"Ah, these are dark and murky days, Poppy. I'll wager that an easterly breeze blowing from the direction of the East India Docks would bring the smoke of ten miles of houses, and at Holloway, a southerly breeze would be filled with the pollution of seven miles or more. The distance to which coal-smoke travels without reaching the ground seems almost infinite. Richmond is just nine miles from here, but views of it are hidden most of the time by the ugly mist. This grey filth reaches to Belgravia and Mayfair now as well.

"Have you ever watched from shore the smoke of steamers passing through the English Channel on a calm day?" he asked.

I nodded.

"The cloud of smoke left behind lies for hours in the same position, like the long, low hand of the Devil. Today, the quantity of smoke is hundreds, perhaps thousands of times greater. There is no escaping it."

"It would seem so. But while your scientific analysis is all very interesting, Sherlock, the only thing that matters to me is that people are very ill because of it, dying of it, and I must try to help them. So thank you for the invitation to lunch, but I shall be on my way now."

"But Poppy, what about the swans?"

My voice shrill, I asked, "What *about* the swans? Or the bees?" I swallowed hard. "I am sorry, Sherlock. I do love the swans and I know you love your bees. But right now *people* are a bit more important to me."

4

As I hurried back to my medical office, I pondered Sherlock's research into the cause of the fog and the illnesses I had been treating all week, but as there was nothing I could do to prevent the fog or eliminate it, the only thing that mattered was how to treat those who came to me for help. The aged, the weak, the infirm suffered most.

A few days before Christmas, my brother Michael had treated three young men, who were out together in the evening. Two immediately fell ill from the effects of the fog and died, and the third had a sharp attack of illness. Deaths from whooping-cough in London were unprecedentedly numerous, almost two hundred. From bronchitis it was far worse. I was no statistician, but the counts at St. Bart's and St. Thomas were close to seven hundred, and of those, two-thirds were likely due to the character of the fog. It was worse than the casualty count after a great battle. Uncle said that the increase in mortality rates at the hospital were more than fifty percent. I'd read a newspaper article earlier in the week that stated:

> It is smoke that makes London fogs
> so mischievous . . . The death-rate during a
> few days of dense fog palpably mounts to an
> extraordinary degree . . . It would be idle to
> doubt that bronchitis and lung-diseases are
> dangerously heightened by moderately thick
> smoke-fogs, when the thickest fogs produce

so great a mortality from those diseases. . .
we must reckon a large annual loss of life
from the perpetual presence in the London
atmosphere of smoke and soot . . . especially
those which happen to be in a weak state of
health, as those recovering from fever.

Surely, I thought, if someone like Sherlock Holmes attacked this dilemma as he did his criminal cases . . . if he would investigate it and determine the exact nature of the 'crime,' he could find a solution. But I highly doubted he had any such inclination.

Much to my surprise, when I arrived at my office near the British Museum, patients stood in a queue that reached down the hallway. I surmised that the range outside the hospital was full, that they had nowhere else to go, and that they had concluded that even a young, female doctor was better than none at all. I did wonder if my brother Michael had sent some of the overflow at the hospital directly to me. I ushered them in and asked them to be seated. Then I set about the business of treating them.

Young and old, male and female, common workers and genteel alike, all presented with symptoms such as I had usually seen only in the chimney sweeps, street sweepers and dustmen. I examined one after another, each complaining of cough and phlegm and dyspnea—difficult or laboured breathing. Upon examination, each one had enlarged airspaces, hyperinflated chests, reduced expiratory breath sounds, and obstructed airways. The causes of bronchitis in those who were not engaged in dusty occupations was clearly the atmospheric and domestic air pollution to which Sherlock referred.

While I could identify the airflow obstruction and inflammation, I was at a loss as to how best to treat it. In medical school, I had read Baillie's *The Morbid Anatomy of Some of the Most Important Parts of the Human Body*, which described and illustrated hyperinflated lungs with enlarged airspaces. Often autopsies of those who died revealed that the lungs did not collapse as they usually do when the air is admitted but remained distended, as if they had lost their power of contracting. I had also read Laënnec's *A Treatise on the Diseases of the Chest*— Laënnec had coined the term emphysema—and *A Treatise on the Diseases of the Chest* by William Stokes of Dublin, Ireland, which included a chapter on emphysema in it. I'd also read all the recently published lectures on emphysema by another doctor, Thomas Hodgkin, a morbid anatomist at Guy's Hospital.

Now, as I examined each patient, I summoned every tidbit I'd learned from Uncle Ormond and everything I'd ever read. The symptoms of bronchitis were cough and expectoration, but what I saw in my patients was the almost complete obstruction of the bronchi, which could become suffocative. Most of my patients complained of dyspnea and in some, the skin had a blue tinge, so I knew they were not getting enough oxygen. The average age for someone who died 'naturally' of bronchitis or emphysema was sixty years. I'd treated patients in my office as young as ten months.

Trying to recall all the suggested remedies in these and other medical texts, I set about my task.

I asked a man in his forties, who said he ran a coffee-stall on Whitechapel Road, what brought him to my office. He said, "One of them boys told me about yer." It could only be Wiggins or one of his little friends, Ollie or Rattle, all errand-boys for Sherlock. He told me that he felt a tightness across his chest, accompanied with a feeling of rawness or soreness and that these feelings were aggravated by every act of coughing. He had a slight fever and a dry cough with very little mucus being expectorated. But during and especially at the end of each act of coughing, he said he felt a painful sensation under the breast bone. He also felt it when breathing in cold air or upon drawing a long breath.

"What remedies have you tried, sir?" I asked.

"At bedtime, a hot foot-bath, a glass of hot toddy and ten grains of Dover's powder."

Dover's was an old preparation comprised of powder of ipecacuanha, a homeopathic medicine, an ingredient in syrup of ipecac used to induce vomiting, powdered opium and potassium sulfate. People also used it to induce sweating, allegedly in advance of a cold and at the beginning of an attack of fever.

Another patient had the same symptoms initially, but then his cough became looser, less painful but more profuse, and it was frothy and streaked with blood. A few days later, the expectoration became thick and yellow, and the cough became more frequent and violent. He had tried using a mustard-plaster to relieve pain and soreness in his chest, and he'd taken to consuming a half-teaspoonful of the syrup of squills every two hours. When he became nauseous, he tried tartar emetic, wild cherry syrup, and water and drank that every two hours. Yet another patient, a man in his fifties who walked very stiffly, had tried nitrate of potash, tincture of digitalis, and syrup of squills mixed with six ounces of water. He said he sipped it every fifteen minutes, but it had done no good.

My roomful of patients had tried many home remedies: garlic, pepper, cinnamon, turpentine, bromides and iodides. I'd had good luck with Kimball White Pine and Tar Cough Syrup, which consisted of four minims of chloroform, so I dispensed this freely. I was concerned, though, because the chloroform could cause fatal cardiac or respiratory arrest, so cautioned my patients about proper dosage.

On the patients with the most advanced symptoms, I tried something that Uncle was employing at the hospital, a vibratory inhibitor administered with a hard-ball applicator. I used short, rapid strokes with medium pressure for about forty seconds to the posterior spinal nerve roots from the seventh cervical to the eighth dorsal.

My last patient of the day was a lovely, young woman with blond ringlets and deep and haunting blue eyes. She was in her mid-twenties and she was dressed in a modest beige blouse and skirt and a dark coat. I guessed that she might be a milliner or seamstress. She presented with symptoms of dyspnea, cough and expectoration and weak breath sounds.

I asked her name.

"Penelope. Penelope Potash. I have a little girl, Miss," she said. "I need to get well to take care of her."

She was skin and bones and also mentioned that her monthly periods had stopped. I'd heard that vibration gave good results for this malady, but I was skeptical about any of these treatments, and particularly this one for absent periods.

"Remove your blouse, please."

As she did so, a strand of sunlight filtered in through the half window, illuminating the dusty desk and creeping across the room. When she turned around, it shone directly on her back. I was aghast at huge bruises, cuts and red welts. I was not sure what instrument of violence was used to beat her, but it would not have surprised me if she also had broken bones or ribs.

I put my hands on her shoulders and turned her round to face me. "What has happened to you? *Who* did this to you?"

She shrugged off my hands, lowered her eyes and said, "I had a disagreement with someone."

"A disagreement! You have welts all over your back. This was not just a disagreement. Who did this to you? We must go to the authorities."

She pulled at her blouse and started to button it.

"No, please. Don't. I'm just trying to help."

She dropped her hands to her sides and averted her eyes again. "I saw something I shouldn't, that's all. This was just his way of encouraging me to keep silent."

"What? What did you see?"

"I can't tell you. Please, can you just give me some medicine?"

I drew in a long breath. I was desperate to find out what had happened to her and put the degenerate behind bars. But I told her I would give her medicine for her bronchial problems and then proceeded to vibrate the nerve roots that supply the uterus, the second, third, fourth lumbar and the second, third and fourth sacral. "This may work," I told her. "But it may not. You need to eat more. You need to be healthy for your monthlies to return."

She shrugged. "I'd just as soon they didn't. One child to care for is enough. And I haven't much of an appetite," she added.

Before she left, she politely requested use of my privy. "It's not very decorous," I told her.

She laughed. "My father was demoted from his profession and forced to clean the urinals at St. James Palace for four shillings a week to make a living. He used to say, 'Royal or not, it all comes out the same.' I don't like to crouch in broad daylight to relieve myself on the pavement. But I don't exactly have a coach with a *bordalou* waiting for me, and I can't afford to buy anything to have the right to use one in a confectioner's or milliner's shop."

It was an unexpected admission from such a well-dressed and well-spoken woman and it made me curious. But I restrained from probing,

She disappeared behind closed doors. When she came out, she thanked me again as I gave her a bottle of ointment for her back and said, "It's too late to apply something cold to your back to ease the swelling. Otherwise, I would send you home with a raw beefsteak that you could eat later."

She smiled and laughed again.

I handed her my scarf to cover her face. She shook her head but I forced it into her hands. "I have another," I told her. "Now, to help with your female problem," I said, "a course of vibratory treatment over sixty to ninety days is usually suggested. Will you come back?"

"What will you charge?"

I had accepted whatever they could give, a shilling here, a pence there, all morning."We'll work something out," I assured her."Now I want you to soak in a hot tub. And then have someone apply this," I said, handing her some ointment. "Dilute it in water first, though, because it can excite irritation in the skin when it's torn and you do have some lacerations."

"What is it?"

"Tincture of arnica. Use some caution with the first application. Will you come back in a few days' time so I may check your progress? And perhaps we can then give you another female treatment."

She nodded. "Yes, yes. I can do that. Thank you. You are very kind."

"And here is some medicine for your breathing."

She wrapped the scarf around her neck. "This is lovely," she said, lifting the edge of the scarf to look more closely at it.

"It was a gift from my aunt. She brought it from France."

"Oh." She started to unwind it and I reached out to touch her hand. "Bring it back when you return."

"I shall, I promise."

"And you'll try to eat better? You will promise that as well?"

She nodded again. "Thank you. Thank you for helping me. And for being so brave."

"Brave?"

"You have the courage to push ahead in a profession that does not welcome women." She tucked the scarf in tightly and added, "But it will be women who do something about this abominable veil of soot, mark my words."

"Twelve hundred died during the Great Fog of December 1873," I said, remembering my uncle's tales about the overcrowded hospital. "And still the factories belch their smoke despite the laws against it."

Though reform has been tried, the domestic hearth still went unchallenged. My father had told me that the year after I was born, 1856, Lord Palmerston introduced the Smoke Nuisance Abatement Act, so mills, factories, printing houses, iron founders . . . most industries were ordered to consume their own smoke as were steam vessels west of London Bridge. But all that changed was the onslaught of litigation.

"The courts hear dozens of cases a year," I said, "but the factories just claim technical problems and households go on unrestricted."

Nodding, she agreed. "Yes, I know. And so London is still a city of smoke and fog. It's clear that sometimes it takes death to force change. Perhaps a few more blokes

27

have to fall off the West India Docks for someone to do something about this noxious smoke that seeps into everything. Maybe it will take a few more deaths for the Queen to—"

She stopped abruptly, and put her hand on the doorknob. "Thank you again, Doctor Stamford. I'll be back for another treatment soon. Oh, and happy Christmas."

"What is your name again, Miss?"

She paused for a long moment and stuttered, "Penelope. Penelope Potash."

"Happy Christmas to you as well, Penelope."

With that, she opened the door and disappeared down the hall. The encounter left me with a sinking feeling in more ways than I could count.

5

It was dinner time when I returned to Uncle's house in Regent's Park. But these days I rose, went to the office, worked, and returned home in darkness, so it was hard to keep mark of the time. Sometimes my biological clock was completely confused by the perpetual night in the Metropolis.

Due to the infernal fog, I often left an extra scarf and gloves at the office, so I'd had an extra scarf to give to Penelope Potash that day. I placed my cape, scarf and hat on the oak coat tree in the hall and dropped my gloves on the table. It was then that I noticed the note from Aunt Susan leaning against the silver bird perched on the rim of the ornate calling card holder on the marble table. I unfolded it and read it; it was dated two days before Christmas.

Happy Christmas, sweet Poppy. As
you, Michael and my stubborn husband
refuse to join us to celebrate at Burleigh
Manor, I've arranged for the Cheadles' cook
to make a proper Christmas dinner. I know
you shall not supply the sustenance.

Of course, I would not prepare dinner. I almost laughed out loud. Sherlock had said once that he could never be a proper husband to me. I was certain I'd never be a normal, suitable wife. I could barely manage to properly steep a pot of tea.

I knew the Cheadle brothers' cook and the men she worked for. They were employed by my uncle's solicitor,

Mr. Havershal. They lived in a run-down century-old home in Holburn, a very tall and ugly edifice that they kept talking about renovating into a law office of their own should they ever leave Mr. Havershal's employ. Their home was dingy with smoke and dirt and sadly in need of a hand of repair. The window frames barely boasted the last remnant of paint and the iron fence was red with rust. Their culinary talents were even less impressive than my own, but they did employ a few servants, one of whom was a plump Irish woman named Fiona McMonagle, who cooked and baked.

I was surprised Mrs. McMonagle had stayed on there for there was no comfort or joy or cosiness in that house. It certainly wasn't gold coins or sterling that kept her there, for though the Cheadle brothers were excellent barristers, very sharp practitioners, they were miserly in the highest degree. She toiled and moiled, but perhaps her pitiable earnestness belied her goal to accumulate enough money before her gray hairs thinned to baldness and her strength failed her. I think she hoped to buy a place of her own, rent out private rooms, and sit, content, by a tiny fire burning in the grate to gladden her spirits, just as Mrs. Hudson did. Mrs. Hudson, Victor Trevor's former housekeeper, had been caught up in a blackmail scheme orchestrated by her husband against Victor's father, but Sherlock had befriended her because of her assistance in bringing that case to a close. Now she owned a building on Baker Street and rented out rooms for an income.

I continued reading Aunt Susan's note as I walked toward the dining room.

*There will be everything from goose
to Christmas pudding and all the trimmings
in between waiting for you when you,
Michael and Ormond have finished your
work for the day. I shall miss you, Poppy.*

> *Love,*
> *Aunt*

Susan.

*P. S. Gifts from your uncle and I are
in the morning room and on the tree.
Presents from your parents, however, are
waiting for you at Burleigh Manor until your
next visit, which my sister urges you to plan
soon!*

I pivoted and turned to walk down the hallway to Aunt Susan's morning room. I surveyed the beautifully-wrapped presents that were stacked on her piano. I sat down at the piano, placed my hands on the keys, and pecked out *The Sussex Carol*, the only Christmas carol I did not fumble over. My hands could hold a scalpel steadily, but my fingers turned into sailor's knots on the ivories. I had almost finished the first stanza when I heard Uncle say, "Happy Christmas, Poppy."

I turned my head and saw him standing near the door. "And to you, Uncle."

He strode across the room and pecked me on the cheek. "You worked rather late."

31

"I had a room full of patients, Uncle. For the very first time! I should be glad of it, but the reasons for it bring me no joy."

"I know," he sighed. "The queue today curled round the hospital and The Square was more crowded than a prison yard during a hanging."

I cringed at the reference. I had attended two hangings with Sherlock and wanted no reminders of those occasions.

"Dinner will be served shortly," he said. "I was amazed Mrs. McMonagle actually found her way through the fog to deliver it. And Genabee is making everything ready for us now."

"I thought Genabee was spending the day with her family."

"She did. But yesterday she kindly offered to help out here this evening. She's a good girl."

And she is not unaware of your kindness and generosity, I thought. She will be compensated handsomely for her loyalty and inconvenience.

"Thank heavens she made it here in one piece," Uncle said. "Most people stayed in today, whether they could have a proper dinner or not. One of the doctors at St. Bart's said the only reason he would have Christmas dinner was because the servants to whom he had given duck and plum pudding were willing to share."

I nodded in understanding. As I had traveled home, I could barely see my hand in front of my face. People were actually asking where they were and house numbers were indecipherable.

"Go wash your face and hands now and come to dinner. Michael and Sherlock are waiting."

"Sherlock? Sherlock is here? But I didn't even hear Little Elihu bark."

Uncle laughed. "Oh, he and Sherlock have become fast friends since your last adventure when that madman attacked the two of you. Elihu saved your lives, remember?"

How could I forget? The serial killer we had tracked down was about to kills us both when my dog sank his teeth into him.

"I invited Sherlock to dinner, Poppy. He was in the lab most of the day and I thought I should see if he had any plans with Mycroft, which he did not. And he was obviously not going home to spend the holiday with Sherrinford and his family. That isn't a problem, is it?"

I shook my head. "Of course not."

"Good. We were just having a port in the library. Now go get ready for dinner."

When he left, I rose to go up to my room, but the array of gifts tempted me. I had to open at least one to brighten my spirits.

I unwrapped a package wrapped in green marbled paper. It contained a curled paper decorated tea caddy. The box was a hexagon with a lid with steel hinges, a brass lock and a brass handle of axe-head form. The top and all the side panels were encased in mahogany banding inlaid with chequered boxwood and ebony. The curled paperwork decoration extended to all the panels with yellow, green and gilt ground contrasting paper and the interior had traces of tea box pewter lining and a base of green woven cloth. A note in Aunt Susan's hand read "For your hope chest."

My hopeless chest, I thought.

I then turned to the smallest box, recalling Sherlock's gift of a locket. Often the finest gifts come in the smallest packages. When I unwrapped it, I found a small wooden keepsake box, the lid of which was decorated in Berlin work, a counted thread design in brilliant shades. Aunt Susan had left another note inside. "To keep your secrets or your fine jewelry . . . as you wish. Now solve the puzzle to find your next gift."

I glanced at the note below. She'd decided to make me play the new game called Doublets, created by Lewis Carroll and recently described in *Vanity Fair*. To play, one had to use several words to change one word into another, using only one letter from the previous word. All the words between the first and the last had to be actual words. As an example, Carroll charged the reader to change the word PIG into the word STY, with five words in between. Aunt Susan did not tell me the last word, though; she'd decided to make it even more difficult. Instead, to find my gift, I had to change the word Noel "into a component of a game, using only Christmas-related words."

My aunt loved such games and she and Uncle were quite good at it, but I had failed miserably each time I tried. Brows furled, my nose in a pinch, I tried for several minutes to work it out. I heard Sherlock say, "What's keeping you, Poppy? I am famished."

I looked up and then held the note out to him. "It's a game Aunt Susan is forcing me to play to find a gift. A riddle of sorts."

He took the note. "Ah, yes. Doublets. I've heard of this." He took a pen from his pocket and scribbled on the back of the note. A few moments later, he said, "Ah! I've got it." He handed the note back to me. He'd written the following words: Noel, Angel, Carol, Song, Sing, King. So he'd taken the 'e' from Noel and used it in the word Angel; then he took the 'a' in Angel and used it in the word Carol. And so on.

"King?" I asked. "But I'm to use only Christmas words."

"Isn't Christ the King? As in King and Queen. Components of the game of chess. I believe you are receiving a chess set. Look there, in the large box on the left."

I quickly opened the largest present. Inside was a beautiful chess set made of ebony and ivory with another note. "You do not do very well on the ebony and ivory in this room. Perhaps you shall excel at this pastime. I look forward to the challenge."It was signed 'Uncle Ormond.'

"Oh!" I cried. "Oh, my heavens. Sherlock, do you play?"

"I have a time or two."

"Splendid. We shall have a game after dinner."

"If you don't hurry along, I shall be dead before your Uncle carves the goose."

I told them about my patients during dinner. "My last patient reminded me of Fantine and Cosette," I said.

"Who?" Sherlock asked.

"The mother and daughter in *Les Miserables*."

He looked totally mystified.

"The novel by Victor Hugo about the French Revolution. Have you not heard of it? It was just published here in London. Fantine is forced into prostitution when she loses her job so that she can support her daughter Cosette. My patient has a little girl. She was as thin as a rail and came to me because of a cough and other symptoms. I am wondering if she has consumption like Fantine did. Maybe I misdiagnosed her. Consumption causes weight loss, fever, and a cough. But I blamed it on the fog."

"Laënnec died from it," Uncle said.

"Laënnec?" Sherlock asked. Suddenly he was interested in the conversation. "The man who invented the stethoscope?"

"Yes, and he used it to support his findings about pulmonary diseases before he died," Uncle explained. "If this young woman is suffering from consumption rather than bronchitis, she needs to go to a sanitorium. One just opened in Falkenstein . . . it's a place where patients can rest and get fresh air and their food intake can be monitored."

"I don't know anything about her, Uncle. She said her name is Penelope Potash but I don't know where she lives. But she promised to return for more vibratory treatments for a female problem."

"Hopefully she will return soon, then," Uncle said. "If she suffers from this illness, time is of the essence."

Then the conversation drifted, of course, to the fog, always the fog.

"I just heard today from my friend Dr. Mitchell." Uncle said. "He's compiling statistics to submit an article to the *Journal of the Scottish Meteorological Society*. The penny post is a marvelous thing, isn't it? We can give each other updates almost daily on statistics regarding mortality rates as well as atmospheric measurements that Sherlock provides. Dr. Angus Smith has been measuring the noxious qualities in the air near Manchester as well. He has an uneasy feeling about the situation."

"I have also," Michael said. "Most expect it to linger for several more weeks. And if the fog does not abate—"

"Many more will die," I croaked, tossing my napkin on my half-eaten dinner.

"I hope that this horrible weather does not adversely affect Her Majesty," Michael said. "She is getting up in years."

"She is but sixty," Sherlock said.

"Which is not young," Michael replied.

"I plan to live to be a hundred. Or forever!" Sherlock answered.

"At any rate, I hope she does not fall ill," Michael said.

"Nor do I," I said. "I do not relish the thought of Prince Edward becoming King just yet."

"You besmirch the Prince?"Michael asked.

"While I wish she had not withdrawn from public life after Prince Albert's death," I said, "it certainly shows the depth of her love and commitment, whereas her son is an adulterer. He has not inherited his mother's moral fiber."

"Poppy!" Uncle said. "Those are rumours."

"Oh, I think it is more than rumour. The prince has built a little love nest for his mistress, Lily Langtry," I retorted. "Oscar Wilde knows her and he told me of this."

Michael shrugged. "They are royalty," he said. "They are different."

"Why? Why are they different? And why should we look the other way? I shall not apologize for the fact that it bothers me that there are so many poor and homeless and wretched on London's streets and the monarchy does so little about it. They are privileged. They are born privileged. I have far more respect for the commoner who pulls himself up by his bootstraps and carves out a living or manages to get a good education despite the odds against it. Like Uncle."

"You have concerns about the prince, Poppy," Uncle said. "About his disregard for his wife's feelings and the Crown's reputation . . . I understand that," Uncle said. "But unfaithfulness does not necessarily equate to an inability to rule justly. Though the Prince may suffer from some moral ambiguity, this does not mean he abandons fairness and justness. People cannot be neatly nor uniformly sorted into kind, tolerant, and trustworthy on one side, and lying, venal, unfaithful and bigoted on the other. Mankind

38

is complex. So the prince's moral deficiencies and his ability to rule are separate issues."

I wanted to agree with Uncle. I loved his humour, his intelligence, his wisdom and kindness . . . his ability to lift you with a word or his capacity to fell you with a look. The intransigence which made him the great surgeon that he was because he settled for nothing less than the highest standard. I loved his ineffable and cynical wit, the clarity with which he saw most things, including me, and the fact that he never spared me the view. I had learned a lot from him. But on this point I disagreed.

"Are they separate issues, Uncle? I think they are linked. I think that one's moral compass guides an individual in all things, and if good judgment is lacking in one place, then it may also be deficient in another."

My dinner companions were saved from further discourse because Genabee brought dessert to the table. I think I saw all three of them heave a sigh of relief.

Sherlock joined me after dinner for a game of chess. I knew the rudiments of the game, but it became clear quite quickly that it would take a long time to excel at it. I admitted this to Sherlock, who said, "To excel in chess is the mark of a scheming mind. You are too altruistic to be much of a schemer, Poppy."

I set about to prove him wrong, of course, but in no time he bested me. He castled the King's rook and announced, "Mate in two moves."

I mentally retraced his last several moves. Uncle undoubtedly would have known how to keep Sherlock from being able to castle on the King's side. With a huff, I laid down my queen and crossed my arms.

"What are you doing?"

"Conceding," I groaned.

He tipped over the king and said, "You don't lay down the queen. You lay down the king. Another game?" he asked, grinning.

I shook my head. "Absolutely not!"

Michael came into the library with two glasses of sherry and handed them to us. He sat down next to Sherlock. "I received a letter from Victor. He heard from a friend of his in the military that things are heating up in Afghanistan. His friend is a doctor who had just set up a charitable dispensary in Kabul. It sounds very bad. Syphilis, leprosy, especially amongst the Hazaras. And many other diseases like asthma. The hospital was ransacked, but we have regained control and apparently it will be up and running again by next month. They have treated a number of wounded as well."

Sherlock abruptly excused himself and I turned to Michael. "What of your friend John? The doctor who went off to Netley last year?" I asked. "Have you heard from him?"

"Oh, yes, Watson. He wrote that he expects to join the 5th Northumberland Fusiliers or the 66th Berkshire Regiment."

Sherlock returned with a small package and gave it to Michael.

"What is this, Sherlock?" Michael asked.

"Something I picked up at Morse Hudson's gallery. A small picture frame. I thought perhaps you could frame a photo for your son."

Michael's face shown his surprise. "That was very thoughtful, Sherlock. Thank you."

Sherlock waved in the air. "Do go on. I did not mean to interrupt."

Michael looked down.

"What is it, Michael?"

"According to my friend John, they are about to deploy to Kandahar. And Ayub Khan hates the British and wants to expel them completely and set himself up as the Amir. Things could get very ugly."

"I shall pray for him."

Perhaps because Sherlock could see that I was uncomfortable with this talk of the war, he said, "Let us not engage in discussion on the follies of mankind over land, religion, title and profit. Poppy, let's talk about the swans."

6

Having no idea what Sherlock was talking about, exhausted from the day and with an early call to duty in the morning, Michael bid us good night and went upstairs to the guest room.

"So," I said, "swans."

"Yes, swans. I finished testing the blood of the swan in the lab. It was, in fact, poisoned before it was slaughtered. The Queen may rest easy tonight. It died a merciful death."

"How so?"

"My chemical analysis revealed the presence of *Datura stramonium*. The swan was drugged with it."

"*Datura* . . . is that deadly nightshade, Sherlock?"

"Yes. *Datura* is a genus of nine species of poisonous vespertine flowering plants which belong to the family *Solanaceae*. It's known as devil's trumpets, moonflowers, Jimsonweed, devil's weed, hell's bells, thornapple, and many more. It's rather like Shakespeare said in *Romeo and Juliet* . . . a rose by any other name."

"You've read *Romeo and Juliet*?" I gasped.

"My mother forced it upon me," he grunted. "I believe the swans were drugged with thornapple."

"Are you sure? Thornapple here? In England?'

"Granted, it is rarely found here. It originates in South and Central America, but it will grow in any open, sunny situation. It flourishes in moderately good soil, but it does best in rich calcareus soil or good sandy loam with leaf mould added. But it has shown up in southern England in rich, waste ground usually near gardens. Sometimes it is planted here in private gardens as an ornamental plant, and it does have a history here, Poppy. It was cultivated in London towards the close of the sixteenth century. In fact," he said, tapping his head while he paused to think, "King Henry VIII was well-known for his medicinal concoctions. This plant may have grown in his herbal gardens. Some may be lurking near the royal household itself. It was often present in gardens devoted to plants used in medieval magic."

"Magic?"

"Yes. As you said, it occurs more rarely herein England. It was first imported from Central America to Italy and then to southwestern Europe. In early times, the thornapple was considered an aid to the incantation of witches, and during the time of the witch and wizard mania here, it was unlucky for anyone to grow it in his garden.

"To some, it can be very appealing, I suppose," he admitted."The buds are a pale, luminous yellow and pure white trumpet flowers when it's in full bloom. The flowers open in the evening and they emit a powerful fragrance."

"Hence, the term deadly nightshade. But wouldn't animals be repelled by the disagreeable odour?"

"Moths are attracted to it but yes, browsing animals would turn away and refuse to eat it. Accidents do occur, however. Children have become deathly ill when they eat the half-ripe seeds, which have a sweet taste. So, if the seeds were mixed with something else or dipped into something . . . what do swans eat?"

"Aquatic vegetation, which they eat while swimming . . . like underwater plants and algae," I explained. "Grasses found along the banks. They will eat small insects and cultivated grains in open fields. People sometimes feed them bread, corn, grain, oats. They like brown rice, lentils, split peas and smallish seeds."

"Seeds," he repeated. "And what would be toxic to them?"

"Chocolate. That can be fatal to a swan. Also salt. Apple seeds because apple seeds contain trace amounts of cyanide. Let's see, what else? Uncooked beans. Mushrooms cause digestive upset, and even liver failure. Caffeine and alcohol. And some stems and vines and leaves are highly toxic. Like the leaves of the nightshade variety. Even tomato leaves are toxic to them."

"So," Sherlock said, rubbing his chin, "if one fed swans the leaves of the thornapple . . . or seeds . . . ."He paused, lost in thought for a moment. "I read one case . . . a child, a toddler, swallowed a hundred seeds. He started to act like an intoxicated person. Then he started to vomit, his pupils dilated, and then he lost his voice and the ability to swallow. He died within twenty-four hours. Another person, an adult, consumed a similar amount and died within seven hours. Another ingested an alcoholic decoction of the seeds and rapidly fell into a coma. So now imagine a very large dose fed to a swan."

"But it's poison. How is that merciful, Sherlock?"

"Because a swan that ingested a large amount of such a concoction would lapse into a coma and die very,

very quickly. I found seeds and leaves throughout the entire length of the intestines."

"Dear God."

"So you see how I have reached my conclusion. I believe that the swan . . . likely all of the swans were poisoned prior to the mutilation. I think first off, the person knows a great deal about the creature. Second, he has access or knows how to gain access; and, third, he does care about them. But he has a grievous dispute with Her Majesty."

"What do we do now?"

"We?" he asked, raising an eyebrow and turning his lips into a gentle smile. "I thought you didn't care about the swans."

"I never said that, Sherlock. The swans are lovely creatures. But I do care more about people."

"I must talk to everyone in Her Majesty's Royal Household," he said. "To the Keeper of the Swans, of course, but everyone else I can interview, everyone from the Master of the Barge to the Paymaster at Buckingham."

"The Paymaster?"

"One Mr. T. C. March, so Mycroft tells me. Who knows? Perhaps someone was shorted his compensation."

"Sherlock, hundreds of people serve in Her Majesty's royal household. You cannot possibly speak to all of them."

"Poppy, I can leave no stone unturned."

"I thought *you* did not care about the swans."

"I do not—*per se*. But it's not about the swans. It is about the *case*, dear Poppy, the case."

45

Over the next several weeks, more dead swans appeared and Sherlock continued to interrogate half the Queen's household. The pernicious effects of the fog lingered still longer, so I continued to treat patients, including the mystery lady who said her name was Penelope Potash, a name I was certain was false because of the way she'd stumbled over it. She came only for the 'female treatments,' as she called them, and claimed her bronchial issues were better, but she was still reed thin and coughed a great deal. I spoke to her about going to a sanitorium or seeking a specialist's help, but she would have none of it. "I don't have Her Majesty's income," she would always reply.

Often as I made my way to and from my office to home, Regent's Park was enshrouded, as if fixed by some supernatural influence. The prodigiously large volume of the deathly mist that floated from every chimney and factory in and near London was held in a kind of thralldom by oleaginous ingredients.

The worst day of all was 26 January, when a thick, slow moving fog draped over the city. Over the next three days, almost twelve thousand lives were lost. In the seven weeks that followed, according to Uncle's friend Dr. Mitchell, the number of fatalities due to the fog was astounding: 1754, 1780, 1900, 2200, 3376, 2495, and 2106.

As I was busy with patients and Sherlock was busy with swans—and, I was about to discover, many other things—I did not see Sherlock again until the end of March when he asked me to have lunch with him. Though the fog had abated to some degree, it was still a struggle to keep the soot from one's clothes. The grime, the obstinate black mixture saturated everything. Uncle had even covered the keyholes of the house with metal plates in an attempt to keep it out.

I did not want to be late, so I set out a bit early to make my way through the pea soup to Simpsons Grand Divan Tavern where I'd agreed to meet Sherlock.

Formerly, it was Simpsons-in-the-Strand, and Sherlock had a penchant for the place these days, because it was well-known as a chess club and coffee house. It had transitioned to the continental preference for haute cuisine, and now boasted lavish décor and a host of waiters. But remnants of its humble beginnings and a plethora of chess memorabilia remained. Master Cook Thomas Davey delighted the customers with his bill of fare, especially wheeling a roast beef to the patrons. In the early days, I'd have been out of place, for this had been a place for gentlemen to smoke cigars with their coffee, browse the daily journals, indulge in long conversations about politics, and sit on the establishment's comfortable divans while they played. Chess matches were played against other coffee houses in the Metropolis and top-hatted runners carried the news of each move. Sherlock called Simpson's a 'poor-man's version" of the Diogenes Club, the private gentleman's club where his brother Mycroft spent much of his time. Mycroft Holmes was the supreme and indispensable brain-trust of the British government, full of government secrets, and we were well aware that the Diogenes was likely some kind of façade at which government officials shared intelligence with those, and only those, in Mycroft's inner circle.

"Not so poor," I'd told him once, referencing the many important people who frequented Simpson's. Charles Dickens used to go there, as did Disraeli, our prime minister, and Gladstone, whose political campaign and series of speeches were **bringing him back into political power.** It occurred to me, as I took a seat across from Sherlock, that he may have suggested lunch at the restaurant not to enjoy the food or the atmosphere of chess but to try to speak with the politicians to find out what they knew about the Royal Swan caper.

Sherlock ordered coffee and a roast beef sandwich, but he wandered away to watch some players engaged in a game. When he came back to the table, he said, "It is a nice set they have there. The pieces on the board are made of rosewood. But it's not a Staunton. Like your Christmas present, the queen has a ball on top without a crown, and the pawns have a button top."

I looked at him, puzzled. "Wait, what is a Staunton?"

"People from all over the world have come to play at this club, Poppy, including Howard Staunton, the world champion. He died just a few years ago. A man named Nathaniel Cooke improved the design of the chess set and called it the Staunton after Howard Staunton.

"I thought you did not care for trivia."

"Oh, not trivial at all, Poppy. The new design is actually based on scientific principles and calculations. Pieces like the ones you have in your set are too tall, easily tip and are cumbersome during play. Some pieces are spindly or top heavy and fall over easily, and because they were so uniform, an initiate to the game, someone unfamiliar with the pieces, can make tragic errors. You see, most chess sets before the Staunton design were confusing because the pieces looked too similar, and that inevitably created mistakes during play, particularly for novices. So, pieces that are universally recognized are important. The Staunton pattern elevates the conventional form. The bases are larger, more stable, and more easily distinguished. The Staunton sets have been around since before I was born. Your chess set is obviously an antique and not nearly as practical to the players. You've really never heard of Staunton?"

"I am not an avid chess player, Sherlock. Just a beginner. As I thought you were."

"Actually, I used to play often with my brothers. Brother Mycroft is quite good—and he never lets me forget it. In fact, although his rails are firmly set in Westminster and he rarely goes anywhere but the Diogenes Club, it wouldn't surprise me if he came round to see the tournaments here. Anyway, some say that the knight in a Staunton set is patterned after the horses of the Elgin Marbles."

"The Elgin Marbles in the British Museum?"

"The same. Some, as I said, believe that the Staunton knight represents the powerful ideas associated with the horses of the Elgin Marbles. Staunton was a Freemason. The sun-god's chariot of On-Helios, as depicted in the Elgin Marbles, is linked to the Egyptian god of resurrection and rebirth, and this is of tantamount importance in Freemasonry."

"So then there's all sorts of Freemason imagery in a chess set?" I asked.

"Yes. For example, the compass on the board reminds us to circumscribe our desires and keep our passions within due bounds. And that is a very sound strategy for living, I should think.

"Did you know that the Freemasons have a volume of The Sacred Laws—the Bible—and the square and the compass symbolise the Ark of the Covenant, which contains laws made by God and agreed to by Man? These were originally kept in King Solomon's Temple, which was 9.14 meters wide and 27.4 meters feet long, and the Staunton pawn has the exact same proportions."

"You amaze me, Sherlock. You really do."

"Why?"

"Because just when I am certain of what you decide to keep and what you decide to purge from that brain of yours, suddenly some trivial fact you have stored comes to the fore."

"Well, all the hours we spent learning about the Buddha and his teachings helped us to solve the British Museum Murders, did they not? This is just another interesting belief system which may come in handy in a case one day."

"Sherlock, why can't you just admit you find the spiritual aspects of Freemasonry and even biblical studies interesting? Why is it that you must always attempt to convince me that you believe in nothing?"

"Not in nothing, Poppy. I believe that it is my duty, like all good citizens, to uphold the law. Sometimes that requires the acquisition of trivial facts. It does clutter the brain. But in any event, my interest in Freemasonry is nothing more than something to store for future cases."

"You must say that lest you be indicted for heresy, because you really do have a moral compass," I laughed. "And have you forgotten that you told me that flowers are our highest assurance of the goodness of Providence? That our powers, desires, food, water and air—these are necessary to exist, but the flower, the rose, is an embellishment, something extra from which we have much hope to gain? Is that not why you brought me the flowers at Holme-Next-the Sea?"

"That again," he scoffed. "A thousand times we could speak of that night in the cottage and still you will not put it into perspective. We were young; we were caught up in our first adventure together; we were inebriated. Yet you persist in it."

I did not feel that way about our night together at the seaside cottage. It was a very special night to me and always would be. "It irritates you, doesn't it? Your lapse in judgement. Or that's how you see it. I suppose I am the thorn, not the rose?"

I was touched by his next gesture. He reached across the table and lightly pressed his fingertips to my wrist. "Never a thorn, Dr. Stamford. But you are, on occasion, as prickly as the thornapple, with its sharp teeth."

I smiled. "*And* its rank, heavy, somewhat nauseating odour, I suppose, as well?"

Now he smiled. "You? Nauseating? Never. Narcotic perhaps," he said, grinning. "And as I recall, a foetid odour arises from the flower *only* when it is bruised," he added. "But generally, the flowers are sweet-scented, remember? They produce a stupor if their exhalations are breathed for any length of time."

I grasped his hand in mine, the fact that we were in public be damned. "And this is why you have always run away from me. Because I do produce some kind of stupor in you. It's why you fight to escape me, isn't it?"

He withdrew his hand and lifted his menu. "I was thinking about religion today, that is all. About religion and about all sets of strong beliefs. Actually, deduction is quite necessary in religion. And the important thing is not to stop questioning. Somewhere out there in this vast world, maybe even within this Metropolis, some like-minded person has been born who, through the science of deduction, who, through being unafraid to ask the right questions, will unleash the great powers of the universe. A great mind, a physicist or the like. I do not believe I shall have that kind of impact on the world, but the science of deduction shall."

I got an eerie feeling. He spoke, just momentarily, as Effie, my dear departed psychic friend, had so many times. She had predicted disasters as well as trivial events. I had never known anyone so prescient. Was Sherlock Holmes being prophetic? Hopeful? Or simply logical?

"Now, we are here to discuss swans," he said, abruptly. "Not Freemasons or flowers or intoxicating scents. I have continued my investigation, of course."

He proceeded to bring me up to date. When I said that Sherlock spoke with half of Her Majesty's Royal Household, I did not exaggerate. He spoke first with the Keeper of the Swans, but he was not helpful. He had fallen ill and was rarely at work or competent to discuss his duties or the case at hand. But Sherlock persevered. By the end of March, he had spoken to over a hundred individuals, including members of the Privy Council; everyone in the Lord Steward's Department; the Duke of Westminster, who was Master of the Horse; Mr. March, the Paymaster; the Earl of Cork, Master of the Buckhounds; the Duke of St. Albans, the Hereditary Grand Falconer; the pages of Honour at the Royal Mews; everyone in the Department of the Mistress of the Robes and those serving with the Groom of the Robes . . . even John Brown, Prince Albert's former ghillie, now the Queen's servant and trusted friend.

But no one seemed to know who was slaughtering the swans or how or why they did it. Not even Sherlock Holmes.

8

I glanced out the window. At times, it was still difficult to see the hansom cabs as they drove by and people moved like ghosts draped in black silk along the pavement. I looked back at Sherlock. "Swans, then. What have your inquiries revealed?"

"Precious little," he sighed. "There are those in dispute with the Queen, of course. Probably thousands throughout England. There are always those who are bitter about the economy or wars or government decisions. But insofar as Her Majesty's Royal Household is concerned, I found no one who had any particular disagreement with the Queen or the Keeper of the Swans. Except perhaps for Gladstone. He and Her Majesty do not get on well. I hear she calls him a Jesuit. His return to government has rather brought to a boil the long-simmering antipathy between the two."

"Well, I hardly think Gladstone is slaughtering swans, Sherlock."

"I agree." He paused and sipped some coffee. "There was a boy I spoke with, though, who was able to enlighten me a bit. His name is Thomas Abnett. He's sixteen or so. He said that they are quite short-handed since the Master and others swanherds have fallen ill."

"And?"

"He mentioned one young man who was practically raised around the swans. His father had been a Deputy Swankeeper for some time but as he aged, he couldn't do the work, so he was given some other menial task to make a living. When he died, the son stayed around for a while but then suddenly disappeared."

"You think this young man might have something to do with all this?"

"Abnett said the boy was very distressed that his father was treated shabbily. But he also thought there was more to it. He'd heard rumours. Something to do with a member of Privy Council and the boy. But he really couldn't tell me more than that."

"You should have Mycroft sift around."

"He is the one who has *me* sifting around. And I do have another matter to which I must attend."

"A new case?"

"Quite so. I shouldn't breathe a word of it, but it will likely be all over the newspapers shortly. It has to do with Wiggins."

"Archie? What has he done?"

"Wiggins has been doing quite well for himself as an entrepreneur—I am told he robs the graves of the poor and sends the corpses to Oxford where dissection is conducted without permission at the medical school."

My inclination was to let out with a wail. Then I remembered where we were and who I was with. But I had feared for some time that Wiggins would take a wrong turn. "Sherlock, did I not inquire about this a few months ago? You mentioned then that you thought Wiggins was traveling down this illegal path."

"Did I?"

"You did. My God, assaults on the privacy of a quiet grave . . . it's despicable."

"Yes. And Wiggins has found himself in quite a quagmire. In the thick of something well beyond his anticipated endeavor. In the process of one of his nighttime ventures, he uncovered a body inside a coffin atop the first tenant. He soon realized that the grave was freshly unearthed and someone had dumped the corpse on top of the original occupant. It seems that someone has committed murder and tried to cover it up by placing body parts in an old grave."

I swallowed hard. "Body *parts*?"

"Wiggins said it was a child's grave, fairly fresh, into which the dismembered adult male was placed."

"Surely Wiggins is not implicated in the murder, is he, Sherlock? He's just a boy."

"He was at first. But I believe I have convinced the authorities that young Wiggins rather did them a favor. Now we just need to find out who the deceased is—which won't be easy, given he was, not unlike our swans, rather savagely mutilated. And then we need to find out who killed him and why."

The waiter had just placed our plates before us. I pushed mine away. Suddenly, I had lost my appetite.

9

Naturally, Sherlock asked me to accompany him to St. Bart's to view the gruesome graveyard find, and he said he had someone he wanted me to meet. We walked because he did not trust a hansom cab in this foul weather—his mother had died in a peculiar and freakish cab accident.

According to Uncle Ormond, the number of cab accidents in the Metropolis had increased ten-fold during the never-ending fog. Uncle urged Bart's to publish the number of injured patients brought to Bart's door, which he estimated at three hundred each week. Sherlock had often said that cab and van drivers considered the roadway as their own property and the people who cross over it as trespassers. When I walked, it was not unusual for a cab driver to shout a 'holloa' at me to get out of the way, never thinking it his duty to avoid hitting a pedestrian by slackening his speed, lest the person be under the horse's feet. Instead, every walker felt he needed to run in order to save his life. Prosecution of these cabmen for furious and reckless driving never seemed to be enforced.

Because of the fog, it took much longer than it should have, close to an hour, to get to Bart's. Sherlock often grabbed my hand to be sure I was still next to him. It was an unexpected comfort. When we passed St. Paul's and finally made our way to Giltspur Street, I breathed a sigh of relief.

"Poppy," he said, "I've been meaning to ask. Have you been to the new wing of the hospital?"

"I've not had the chance, Sherlock. Uncle was at the opening ceremony in November, though. He said that the

Prince and Princess of Wales dedicated the new building. But it isn't finished yet, is it?"

"Not all of it, but much of the construction is completed and it should be done in time for the opening of the winter session on October 1st. I am looking forward to it—especially the new dissecting room."

St. Bart's had been serving the people of London since the twelfth century. It had, of course, changed a great deal over the years. But the new wing was the grandest and loftiest in its evolution.

The new wing would be comprised of a museum; classrooms; a physiological laboratory, a library, anatomical, pathological, and pharmaceutical laboratories, each two or three times larger than the old ones. The students already had been warned that the new library would not be a place for lounging, talking and letter writing. Its purpose was for study. No *Punch, Graphic* or *Field* magazines would be permitted within its walls. Strict silence was to be enforced, 'just like Mycroft's Diogenes Club,' Sherlock told me, and only industrious students would be welcomed into its quiet recesses.

The basement floor would house two classrooms, a lavatory, a more commodious cloak room and locker rooms—so Uncle told me though I was sure I'd never see them. One classroom was for bone classes and the other for The Abernethian Society, whose members discussed new methods of treatment, presented papers on interesting subjects . . . and read *Punch* when no one was looking. A moveable wood partition would divide the physiological laboratory into a large room and a small one. My uncle's good friend, Dr. Harris, had been appointed to Director of the physiological lab. The smaller of the rooms would be devoted to research by vivisection.

I was not surprised that the room that most excited Sherlock was the large dissection room. Situated on the site of the old museum and the old dissection room, it was to be fitted with the latest equipment for the study of anatomy and the osteological department of that study. Students would no longer need to repair from the dissection room to the museum for the purpose of grounding their knowledge of studying bones. The plans included a large gallery which would encircle the new dissection room and on each side of it would be mounted the most perfect osteological specimens available, affixed so that they could be turned about in any direction without being handled or removed from their place. It would have its own special heating apparatus so that students could dissect during the winter months without having to wear coats or take time to visit the fireplace. A lavatory had been installed next to the dissecting room, as well as a special room for demonstrators and prosectors and two locker rooms. The anatomical theater would seat 520 men and the new medical theater had a capacity of nearly three hundred. It was modern and convenient for the students in every way. Even a covered walkway from the library to the new block was under construction.

When we arrived at the entrance to the new wing, Sherlock ushered me inside and we made our way to the shell of the gallery of the anatomical theater. He said, "The gentleman to whom I shall introduce you, Frederick Womack, is an acquaintance of mine, a brilliant young medical student. He has some fascinating ideas. Though he is only a third-year, he has received many high honours. He is experimenting with pin-pointing time of death. He believes that soon we shall be able to accurately report the time of death to the minute."

"Temperature calculations?"

"Womack is inventing a special mercury thermometer with a flattened bulb of thin glass. He intends to attach the thermometer to the cadaver's belly and take temperature readings that will calculate postmortem interval with extreme accuracy."

"My goodness. That would be quite an invention."

"One day, I'm certain that he will be a teaching fellow and perform his temperature calculations in the mortuary and in this Anatomical Theater. There he is," Sherlock said, pointing.

Once we were within earshot of Mr. Womack, I realized that he was talking with someone I knew, Jonathan Younger, who had attended the Harrow School with my brother Michael. He had served as Michael's best man. Jonathan and Mr. Womack were discussing St. Bart's most recent football season and Bart's loss to the Harlequins at

Turnham Green. I heard Jonathan say, "After Bart's first loss to the Harlequins—you remember they scored one goal and one try to nil—I thought the season was over."

"Yes," Womack said, "that same day they played again at Forest Gate against Upton Park and lost there as well."

"But what a turnaround. In the second match of the Cup Ties at Clapham Rovers, they gave Guy's the old heave-ho."

Finally, the two men noticed us. Womack turned and said, "Ah, Sherlock, what do you think of the hospital's football team?"

"I don't think about it at all, Frederick. May I present Dr. Poppy Stamford? Poppy, this is Frederick Womack."

The two men standing before me could not have been more different. Frederick was short and dark with glasses. Jonathan was an extremely attractive young man— tall and athletic with flaxen hair, violet eyes and a sunny smile.

Frederick gave me a little bow and said, "A pleasure, Miss," but Jonathan rushed forward to give me an unexpected hug. "Poppy, how wonderful to see you."

It occurred to me that Sherlock had not been to Michael and Effie's wedding and he generally stayed in the lab, did not socialize and had few friends. So he likely did not know Jonathan. "Pardon me," I said, "I believe I have overlooked an introduction. Sherlock, this is Dr. Jonathan Younger. Jonathan, Sherlock Holmes."

"Ah, so you are the unauthorized, eccentric occupant of our lab, then," Jonathan exclaimed. "Michael mentioned you just the other day. Some sort of detective, are you?"

"A consulting detective," Sherlock said with a grimace.

"Poppy," Jonathan said, "I don't believe I have had the pleasure of seeing you since Michael and Effie's wedding, or perhaps it was at her funer—" He stopped mid-sentence.

I had not seen him since Effie's funeral.

"Yes, I believe it's been well over a year, Dr. Younger. It's wonderful to see you. You're looking well."

"As are you," he said. "And call me Jonathan, for heaven's sake." He looked at Frederick. "I've known Dr. Stamford—both Dr. Stamfords—since childhood. I was her brother's roommate at Harrow."

"So you know each other well?" Sherlock asked.

Before I could answer, Jonathan said, "Very well. And you, Poppy, what do you think of St. Bart's victory over its old enemy, Guy's Hospital?"

I shrugged.

He turned back to Womack. "I must say, we showed our voice with such patriotism that we drowned out the feeble cries of Guy's. It was a brilliant victory." His whole body animated and contorting it into football moves and gestures, he continued. "Bart's won the toss and kicked against the wind. Uphill, they forced to a touchdown once, and then, just before half-time, they worked the ball, inch-by-inch to the enemy's line and Ray obtained a try. After half-time, it was Bart's again. They scored fast and Roberts obtained the ball, and in a beautiful run, he carried it right behind Guy's post and the try was converted to a goal." Jonathan's face was almost effervescent as he recounted the last moments of the game. "Guy's made a valiant effort, I must concede, but Roberts got the ball once again, made the best run of the game, and obtained a third and last try.

"When time was called, the game stood Bart's one goal, two tries, three touchdowns, to Guy's one touchdown. Roberts—" He looked at me and offered as an aside, "Roberts is the quarterback. He was remarkable, but all the forwards were grand, particularly Faddy, Sales and Llewellyn. Oh, and J. Pemberton Campbell. He was stupendous."

"Isn't Campbell the one who's seeking an appointment as resident surgeon to Dr. Joseph Bell at the Royal Infirmary in Scotland?" Womack asked.

"The same," Jonathan said. He turned to me again and said, "After the game, we hoisted Roberts and carried him in triumph from the field amid cries that would rival a flock of sheep!"

I laughed. Jonathan reminded me of my brother—an avid football fan—and also of Cuthbert Ottaway, one of Oxford's finest former athletes, Ottaway was also fair and handsome and he had quite the magnetic personality. I chanced to meet him on the same day I'd met Sherlock while I was attending the final rowing contest of Eights Week. Jonathan's features and coloring were similar. However, I hoped Jonathan had a more prosperous future. Cuthbert's brilliant future and promising career in law had been cut short far too soon. He had contracted pneumonia and died at the age of twenty-seven, just a year ago.

These memories prompted me to ask, "How did Oxford fare last week in the rowing race? The races have just begun, have they not?"

"You didn't know?" Jonathan asked. "The fog last Saturday was too impenetrable for the race to be rowed at the fixed time. All the rowing on the ebbtide was abandoned. With the weather as it's been, it is no surprise. But they did finally have a go at it on the following Monday, and Oxford did herself proud. I suppose I am a malcontent with nothing to soothe my soul now that Oxford reckons two wins more than the light blue colors."

"You went to *Cambridge*?" Sherlock shrieked.

"Indeed."

"But not Eton, Sherlock," I said quickly. "So he is not altogether doomed to the Sixth Circle of Hell."

"I think Dante would disagree," Sherlock mumbled. "The Sixth Circle is reserved for heretics, so surely there is at least a half-circle in the Inferno for Cambridge alumni, even if they did not attend Eton."

Jonathan laughed uproariously. Then he asked, "So what brings you here, Poppy? Are you taking a tour of the new facilities? You must see the new Abernethian Room. Very cheerful with comfortable leather-cushioned seats round the walls and a large table with writing materials and newspapers and monthlies. A lovely place to lounge."

He and Womack prattled on about one of their physiology professors and I saw Sherlock begin to fidget. Then Jonathan turned to me again and abruptly changed the subject. "Poppy, have you heard that there is an opening for a Junior Assistant Medical Officer to the Surrey County Lunatic Asylum near Wandsworth-common Railway Station?" he asked.

I shook my head.

"Oh, but never mind. I think they probably don't want a—" He paused and stuttered. "But . . . but there's . . . there's also a vacancy for a House Surgeon to the Carmarthn Infirmary The advertisement in the Hospital Gazette said that candidates must be unmarried, know the Welsh language and submit testimonials."

"I don't know Welsh, Jonathan."

"Too bad. I was just thinking it might be a fresh start for you, Poppy. They might not care that you are a female. Then again, the candidate must also be a member of the College of Royal Surgeons who don't admit—" He stopped and looked down.

Who don't admit women, I thought.

"You see, I just thought . . . well, Michael told me that your practice is barely surviving."

Sherlock clenched his fist at his side. "Her practice is surviving very well, sir. Have you not noticed the fog outside? Patients are beating down the doors to Dr. Stamford's medical office. She is a good doctor, a staunch practitioner, and does the best she can to wrest the country from the quicksand in which it is drifting at present."

Jonathan glanced from Sherlock to me and back again. "Forgive me. I do apologize. I meant no disrespect. So, you have been treating patients for asthma and dropsy, I presume?"

65

I nodded yet again.

"Are you treating your patients with morphia for the dyspnea?" Jonathan asked. "There is a strong belief that employment of hypodermic injections of the drug can rapidly cure some attack. And opium is a useful drug as well; it relieves bronchial spasms . . . though I understand it's rather useless in emphysema."

This launched a protracted discussion about the treatment of patients with fog-related symptoms, and I saw Sherlock's agitation and impatience rising. He wandered away and disappeared for a time.

When he returned, Jonathan had just turned our discussion to the Tay Bridge Disaster of 28 December in Scotland. During a violent storm, one that some termed a hurricane, the Tay Bridge had collapsed while a train travelling from Wormit to Dundee was passing over it, killing all aboard.

"The way I understand it, the piers were narrower and their cross-bracing was less robust than on prior bridges designed by Sir Bouch," Jonathan explained. "Apparently, he made no allowance for wind-loading, and there were other flaws in the design of the bridge as well. I heard that only forty-six bodies of the fifty-seven who perished were recovered."

I sighed. So once again, I thought, a new year had dawned on weeping families, mourning for friends and dear ones, just like those who had been left behind after the two train collisions in December of 1874—collisions where Uncle and I had tended to the wounded. In one swift moment, a fraction of a second, passengers were torn from a pleasant excursion and thrust into the grim reality of death. I could hear them crying out, their voices drowned out by the howling storm, their pleas for help muted by the rising tide. Their families would have to live with the fact they were carried out to sea, never to be seen again, never to be given a proper burial. A feeling of horror arose in me with memories of the Norfolk tragedies I had personally witnessed.

Sherlock gave Jonathan a stern look and said, "Please, Dr. Younger, spare us the details. Dr. Stamford has herself rendered care to railway and other disaster victims. As has her brother Michael, which I would think you would know if you were truly his friend. Have we all not had enough during this most unfortunate period of gloomy death and disease and war and trouble? Must you bring forth more dread tidings?"

I touched Sherlock's arm. "It's all right, Sherlock."

He offered his elbow and abruptly turned about, dragging me with him. "Excuse us, gentlemen. We have an appointment with a corpse."

10

Once we were in the lab, Sherlock loosened his tie and tossed his coat and waistcoat over a chair. "Younger is impertinent."

"No, he isn't," I protested, as I removed my cape, scarf, gloves and bonnet. "I've known him for years. He's very sweet and quite gregarious."

"I must disagree. There is compelling evidence to the contrary. He is obnoxious and condescending and you should have nothing more to do with him."

I had had enough of Sherlock's possessive nature, I truly had. Though he refused to give into his affection for me, he was ever-so covetous of my time. I'd finally grown tired of languishing in self-pity and sick of trying to convince him that we were right for each other. I did still love him, but I had shed an ocean full of tears. I had spent endless nights mourning our summer tryst, and I was desperately trying to move on.

"Sherlock! What is wrong with you? Has your brain been suddenly inundated by a feast of toxic particles of the fog? Do dispatch a regiment of gluttonous warriors from that cold heart of yours to gobble the poisons and recapture your senses. Jealousy does not suit you."

"What?"

"If you allow your heart to feel, I fear that your other organs, including your brain, may soon deteriorate and stop functioning," I snarled.

"Don't be ridiculous. I simply meant that he offended you."

"You have no right to decide if I am offended."

"He belittled you," he bellowed. "Taunting you with posts to which your application would be futile and disparaging your now flourishing practice."

"Flourishing for the time being, but only because of the fog and because people cannot afford to go elsewhere. My practice may not survive, Sherlock. I must concede that."

"Concede nothing!" he shouted. "You are a brilliant woman. I would not keep you in my company were that not the case."

"Fine."

"Fine," he repeated. "Now let's have a look at our unnamed corpse, shall we?"

As I viewed the unattached parts of the poor soul, Sherlock read to me an advertisement that had appeared in a recent edition of *The Students Journal and Hospital Gazette*.

> Fresh botanical specimens and other seasonable plants, including Aconite, Belladonna, Conium, etc. (likely to be seen at examinations during the summer months) Carriage paid. 5s. per set; singly, 8d each— Saunders, Private Tutor, 79, Gaisford Street, N.W.

"What do you think of that?" he asked.

"I think it's clear that anyone with a few shillings can get his hands on deadly nightshade, even if none is growing in the area."

"Precisely. Poison with which to kill the swans. Perhaps I should answer this advertisement to see how easily one might acquire the poison. Now do see what you can tell me about this body."

I looked at the body parts and clothing laid out before me. The deceased had been found dressed in top hat and tails and none of it had disintegrated. The gentleman had not been dead long; there was little evidence of decomposition of the remains. The head had been severed from the torso, as had the legs and arms. The man was in his early forties, white, and well-nourished.

"This was not done with a hatchet or saw, Sherlock. Whoever cut up this body has surgical training. Where was the body found?"

"St. Marylebone Cemetery in East Finchley. This grave was very near the grave of Sir George Hayter, Her Majesty's principal painter in ordinary. He was buried there just a few years ago."

"I know of it. My Aunt Susan's grandparents are buried there. The parish boundary stone is in Regent's Park."

"Did you know that The Non-Conformist Chapel was opened there in 1854, the year of my birth, as a Dissenter's mortuary chapel? I find that appropriate."

I stared at him in disbelief. I was bewildered at times at how such a focused mind could wander into totally unrelated discourse. Sensing my impatience, he said, "At

70

any rate, this is not where Wiggins was customarily sent to exhume bodies. He generally went to pauper's fields and hospital cemeteries. He had an arrangement to get the bodies to Oxford by train, but this time he was apprehended by a constable."

"Sherlock, they don't even have a proper medical school at Oxford yet. On the grounds, I mean. There is an infirmary, which Michael says is well-arranged and equipped, and there are instructors, like the Regius Professor of Medicine, but the students have to go off campus. They cannot even spend much time at the Radcliffe Library because at the same time they are prosecuting their studies elsewhere."

"True. There were some twenty-five hundred undergraduates last year, but only sixty have graduated in medicine thus far," he said. "Dr. Ackland was always lobbying for more money for the school. He said that in the absence of a true medical school, there is a blight on the University's reputation and he sought to restore the ancient prestige of Oxford."

"Michael told me that he resigned his position at the Radcliffe Infirmary last year because there is no real medical school and his position was nothing more than a sinecure. And from what I understand, Oxford has a dearth of cadaver specimens for its medical students to study."

"As does Bart's, for that matter," Sherlock said.

"But I thought the wretched Resurrectionists were finished. Isn't that why Parliament passed the Anatomy Act years ago? To prevent body-snatching for payment?"

71

"Yes, but Mycroft says that because the schools do not have enough cadavers for pupils and surgeons to dissect, there are rumours that even the Royal London Hospital has resorted to obtaining specimens from the hospital's own burial grounds—in other words, former patients. I'd wager that if an investigation were undertaken, we'd find that some coffins have more than one occupant, and there would be fewer bodies than heads. Think about it. If, during the winter, the medical professors and surgeons keep all who die under their care, then in the summer they have enough and some to spare. But during the summer months, it is difficult to preserve subjects. They inject a solution of arsenic and chloride of zinc or glycerin, but now, under the law, bodies can only be kept for eight weeks."

"This is a gruesome situation," I said. "Oxford is full of medical scandals, it would seem. The coroner there, Mr. Hussy, acts like an old woman. He didn't call in the House Surgeon when someone died at the infirmary a few weeks ago; he called a visiting surgeon who refused to come. Hussy does this every time there is a fatality—probably because the House Surgeon thinks half the time Hussy cannot do his job. But robbing graves?"

"Actually, I think Hussy is trying to do his job. It is not just unclaimed bodies that are used for anatomical research and to train medical students. People prey on the poor, Poppy."

"What do you mean?"

"They talk guardians into contracting for the bodies of loved ones—people in workhouses and the like," he explained. "The staff at Radcliffe Infirmary have a particularly disdainful attitude toward the poor. Just this year, there was a terrible scandal about the dissection of pauper corpses and contracts with relatives. There has been a tug-of-war over which bodies end up in the Dead House and how they get there, who pays for the coffin, and so on. There's all sorts of back-door trading at the infirmary. Medical students, professors and researchers are definitely involved in the body-buying trade. And it *is* a covert trade, Poppy, a despicable one in which many are involved. The deceased, the relatives, the railway, with tips to porters who look the other way when hearse drivers deliver cadavers. Do you realize we are in a recession and that a deceased infant's body can earn poor relatives a year's wage and save the cost of a funeral?"

I felt overwhelmed with it all. Finally I said, "But *this* body, Sherlock. This body was found in a London church cemetery". I thought for a moment. "Sherlock, is there anyone connected to Oxford who is missing? Someone who may have found out that Wiggins was sending bodies there and wanted it ceased? Was Wiggins confronted with anyone or—?"

"Don't get ahead of yourself, Poppy."

"Does Wiggins know the name of his benefactor? The person paying him for the bodies?"

"No. He went to the Fortune of War public house in Smithfield on Pie Corner every Friday night to wait for instructions."

"I don't understand, Sherlock."

73

"Once upon a time," he said, "there was a room in the back of the public house with benches with the grave robbers' names. They waited there with specimens, and surgeons at St. Bart's came there to appraise the cadavers. Despite the change in the law regarding grave-robbing, it is a practice that continues. But here's the thing. I don't believe that a true anatomist would engage in this particular type of supply. Mycroft did say that Oxford and Cambridge coordinate activities. Usually, they buy from the poorest areas of the city and apparently they also walk the streets to establish body-buying networks. From what I understand, body parts are thrown into the river or a clinical waste bin. But this enterprise seems different. Wiggins has robbed criminal graves and hospital graves, but never from a place such as St. Marylebone. He did mention that the note sent to him to dig up this particular grave and await further instructions was written in a different hand. He was not sure it came from his usual benefactor. I must speak to him again about that."

My uncle had, for many years, kept a running diary of events and staff at the hospital—a venerable history of the place. I wondered if he had noted these enterprises anywhere in his writings.

"I am in the process of getting more information," Sherlock said. "Inspector Hopkins is the one who asked me to look into this. You remember Hopkins?"

"Of course." Stanley Hopkins, Sr. was with the Yard, a dedicated man who had assisted us in obtaining the evidence to send the British Museum murderer to the gallows.

"You recall his keen interest in Phrenology?"

"Yes."

It was Hopkins' one peculiar trait. Those who promulgated phrenology believed that by examining the shape and unevenness of a head or skull, one could discover the development of the particular cerebral "organs" responsible for different intellectual aptitudes and character traits. For example, a prominent protuberance in the forehead at the position attributed to the organ of Benevolence indicates the individual has a "well developed" organ of Benevolence and would therefore be expected to exhibit benevolent behaviour.

"According to Hopkins," Sherlock continued, "there are still people trying to prove that theory. Hopkins thinks there could be some relationship to such a person. Have you heard of Lombroso? He says criminals are evolutionary throwbacks that we can recognize by the shape of their jaws or cheekbones or the length of their arms. He argues that these individual's physical traits come with some intrinsic craving for evil, and a desire to kill and mutilate. Even to drink blood from a corpse."

"Vampires," I said.

"Exactly. Nonsense," he muttered.

"The last time I saw Oscar Wilde, he told me that his ex-fiancée's new husband, Bram Stoker, is researching European folklore about that for some kind of novel. Oscar said that in Romanian myths, the *strigoi* are troubled souls who rise from the grave and have magical powers. Sounds like something from a Penny Dreadful." I smiled to myself. "Oscar also said that Stokes' actor friend—the one who set up Stokes as manager of his theater—would be a good model for the character. But I told him it's already been done. That book by John Polidori introduced a very aristocratic man as a vampire."

He stared at me as if I'd lost my mind, prattling on and on about vampire stories. "Yes, you're right. I digress," I said, knowing he was now the one who was impatient with a subject in which he had no interest, particularly as it related to Oscar Wilde, cousin to my brother's late wife, for whom Sherlock had little use. "So tell me, Sherlock, what does this man's murder have to do with phrenology?"

"Hopkins is in some group that meets to discuss the topic," Sherlock said. "He said he has heard—and mind you, it is all conjecture—that there is a medical professor at Oxford who is trying to prove these theories. His name is Danford Hopgood. He could be the one paying Wiggins to rob the graves for specimens. Wiggins said he dug up quite a few criminals at the specific request of an anonymous benefactor, this one included. And Hopkins says that the professor has not been seen for days . . . but this dead man is *not* the professor. Hopkins described him as very slightly built, reed-thin, and balding. This disembodied individual does not fit that description."

"And could a professor afford this sordid enterprise?" I recalled that Effie's father, a professor at Oxford, could not even afford the wedding dress she so desired. "I don't think so."

"Mycroft has spoken to everyone in the anatomy department at Oxford and other people of influence there. It appears the supply of cadavers does come from nearby workhouses and the poor, but not from the cemetery where Wiggins was instructed to dig."

"What if—" I paused a moment to think. "What if this man before us, who obviously is of some social standing, assuming, of course, the clothing was not stolen to lead authorities even more astray should the corpse be discovered . . . what if he were connected somehow to this grave robbing scheme at Oxford? If a professor wanted specimens to study in an area outside of the normal course of human anatomy, to prove some theory, he would need funding, would he not?"

"This could be the real benefactor of the whole scheme, you mean," Sherlock said. "Funding the professor's research."

I nodded. "Someone who perhaps decided to withdraw his funds. Or it could be someone who wanted to stop the research."

"That would be motive," Sherlock exclaimed.

He threw out his arms and brought his hands together in a clap. "Ah, Poppy, the game's afoot. I shall meet with Hopkins at once to see if he can track down a list of the professor's benefactors."

He put his hands on my shoulders. "You see? I told you that you are brilliant."

11

To my surprise, Jonathan was loitering outside the lab when I emerged. Donning my gloves, I said hello.

He smiled. "Poppy, I'm glad I caught you. I ran into Michael and I was hoping you'd still be here. I was just wondering . . . ." He paused.

"Yes? You were wondering? What? Why I spend so much time in the company of Sherlock Holmes, I suppose?"

"Yes. Well, yes, that, but I didn't mean that. I was wondering if there is someone from whom I should ask permission to take you to dinner."

I took a step backward. "Dinner?"

"Yes, dinner," he laughed. "Your parents are in Norfolk, but I know you live in the care of your aunt and uncle. Should I request permission from Dr. Sacker?"

I was literally too stunned to reply.

"I mean, I realize," he continued, "that you are not a child and that you have your own mind on everything from medicine to politics. You don't strike me as one who romanticizes love or feels some need to adhere to customs like being chaperoned or engaging silly masquerades like flirting with your fan."

If I were inclined to indulge in such silly rituals, I thought, what message would my fan be sending right now? *Leave me be*? Or *I'm independent*? Or *I'm flattered*? I don't think I knew.

"You are right, Jonathan, I do not."

"Good, because I have never been able to make much sense of these flirtatious signals. For example,

78

swinging a fan or leaving it half open or shutting it abruptly." He waved his right hand through the air as if cooling himself with a fan. "What a woman means by all that is lost on me. You have always been very direct. So, pray, tell me, would you be so inclined to have dinner with me if I properly request permission from your Uncle?"

I thought for a moment. What would Mum and Papa or Uncle and Aunt Susan think of Dr. Jonathan Younger? My parents had always liked Jonathan; they would be ecstatic to learn of his interest in me. My mother, in particular, was anxious for me to find a husband and Jonathan was just the sort of man she had in mind.

We were certainly within the same so-called class, although in reality, he was rather above my status. His family had a grand estate, just miles from our own. His cousin was an Assistant Master in the Classics at Harrow. His grandfather had been a Knight Exalted of the Most Noble Order of the Garter and of the Most Distinguished Order of St. Michael and St. George, due to his service in the Napoleonic Wars. His uncle was a Marquis.

"Well, Poppy?"

"I am a bit . . . a bit confused by your sudden display of interest, Jonathan. We have known each other a long time . . . and you and I spent a lot of time together during the pre-nuptial activities and at Michael and Effie's wedding . . . the better part of a week. But I detected no particular attentiveness on your part toward me. In fact, I believe you were practically engaged to a young woman named Flora Codrington. The daughter of one of her Majesty's ladies in waiting."

"Her mother attends Princess Beatrice, actually. But Flora is . . . how shall I say it? A bit dull. Slightly dim-witted."

If that were the case, and given the fact that gentlemen like Jonathan rarely cared for women whose intelligence had been encouraged, it surprised me that he and Flora were not already wed with three children.

"You have a keen mind, Poppy. You are progressive. It rather . . . it rather excites me."

I considered his proposal and blurted out, "I would consider sharing a meal with you, Jonathan. Perhaps lunch. And there is no need to request permission of my uncle for that."

"I'd hoped for dinner. Perhaps before going to the theater. Or after a day at Rosherville Gardens."

Again, difficult memories made their way to the fore. A favorite steamboat, the *Princess Alice*, running a pleasure cruise from London to the Rosherville Gardens at Gravesend, had sunk not long ago, and I still lamented the seven hundred lost lives, many from the pollution in the Thames rather than drowning. I'd treated the survivors. I had not saved many.

"It is only March, Jonathan, so the gardens are not open to the public yet." I took a deep breath and said, "However, I will agree to have lunch with you. Perhaps tomorrow? You may decide the when and where and send a page this evening to Uncle's with the particulars. Good day."

I turned to leave and he touched my shoulder. "It really was a lovely surprise, running into you today." Then he stepped aside to let me pass.

I smiled and started down the hallway. He called out, "Have a wonderful day, Poppy!"

Puzzled and perplexed, a little shaken and even a little intrigued, I hurried back to my office.

As the sun had come out from behind the grizzled clouds and the fog had thinned, I took my time going back to my office, so that I could think. I had surprised myself, accepting Jonathan's invitation to dine with him.

I stopped at Lowther Arcade opposite Charing Cross Station, a bazaar where mosaic jewelry, toys and such were sold, and picked up a few things for little Billy, Wiggins brother. Then I found myself on Pall Mall near the Diogenes Club, where Sherlock's brother Mycroft spent most of his waking hours and where I'd met with him in secret when he enlisted me to help ferret out some of Britain's most heinous criminals—baby farmers.

Pall Mall was the heart and lungs of British aristocracy and social advantage, where English gentlemen found their pleasure in quiet discourse. It was like a street of palaces, the clubs being frequented by political celebrities and government officials. It stood out for another reason. Most of London's most stately building were Gothic in style, but the clubs of Pall Mall were classical to one degree or another. The Reform was Italian, the Carlton next door more florid. Though it was but a stone's throw away, Marlborough House could not be seen from the street and this was the residence of the Prince of Wales, which stood within the walls of St. James Palace. When meeting with Mycroft during the course of the baby farming investigation, I had often wondered if afterward he had scurried straight over to Marlborough to enlighten the prince as to the progress of our investigation. Next to Marlborough came Beaconsfield, the Guards, the Oxford, the Cambridge, the Carlton, the Reform, the Travellers, the Athaeneum, the Wanderers, and the Kennel. And, of course, Mycroft's Diogenes, which stood just before Charing Cross, a short walk from Whitehall, the pulse of British government.

I was about to head toward the Strand to make my way back to the office when a cyclist sped past me, skittered by a few other pedestrians, wobbled and very nearly collided with an enormous man whose girth almost filled the entire walkway. I realized it was Mycroft Holmes.

He shouted at the boy and spun around, a feat which must have taken great effort, and shouted again. As I came almost face to face with him, he grumbled, "Damn bicyclists. They totally disregard the safety of others. The prejudice against them shall only be fostered and increased by these feverish riders who needlessly put members of the public in harm's way. Infernal machines."

I grinned. "Good day, Mr. Holmes."

Finally, he tipped his hat to me and said, "Dr. Stamford." The he added, "Damn cyclists."

Remembering how Effie and I would ride quite recklessly through the grounds at Oxford, often barely avoiding passersby, I could not resist needling him. "Uncle told me that there is a Bicycle Union now, organised to protect the rights of bicyclists and to watch the legislation of Parliament that might affect the interests of the bicycling public."

"Yes," he scoffed. "But do the cyclists that the Council of the Union seek to protect heed any of the regulations and principles recommended to thwart altercations on the roadway? I tell you, they do not. These maniacs best be mindful of them. There was a case just last year, heard by Justices Lush and Mellor . . . *Taylor v. Goodwin*, I believe it was . . . that case imposed great penalties for furious and irresponsible driving. I do not see why we have allowed these strange beasts to invade the streets."

I lifted my scarf to cover the wide smile on my lips. Anything akin to exercise was most foreign to Mycroft Holmes, as was most evident by his ever-widening waistline. Much like Oscar Wilde, who would rather hail a hansom to cross the street, Mycroft held physical exertion in disdain.

"I take it you are on your way to the Diogenes? Or Whitehall? Busy with work as usual?"

"In Her Majesty's service, as always, Dr. Stamford. But I am glad I have bumped into you."

"Me, rather than the cyclist?" I quipped.

He scoffed. "Yes, yes, well . . . I sent a page to find Sherlock but he is not at home nor is he anywhere to be found at St. Bart's."

"I just left him; he did not mention that he had any appointments."

"Well, it's most important I find him. He has once again interjected himself into police business."

"It is my understanding that Hopkins asked him to help."

He raised an eyebrow. "Well, we have no need of his help," he scoffed. "We have identified the mutilated corpse."

I canted my head to look at him more closely. Though in many ways they were alike, there was an inexplicable and sometimes bitter enmity that burned between them. Often harsh words were exchanged,

"Have you? Who is it then?"

"A member of the Privy Council."

"Really? Sherlock said that no one was reported missing."

"His wife . . . widow, now . . . just appeared at the Yard a few hours ago. She said that he went to some kind of formal affair two nights ago and did not come home."

"Two nights? And she did not worry about his whereabouts?"

He tilted his head side to side. "I did not inquire about the state of their marriage, but she volunteered that it was not unusual for him to disappear from time to time. However, this time she felt uneasy. They recently lost a child—some kind of bronchial infection due to this

84

unrelenting fog—and he has been more attentive to her needs and emotive outbursts than previously."

"Mycroft, Sherlock thinks there is some connection between the man found in the child's grave and a grave robbing scheme. Young Wiggins was specifically instructed to dig up that grave."

"So I am told. Dr. Stamford, have you any idea where Sherlock may have gone? This is a sordid business. Could be quite dangerous."

I felt my breath hitch. I should have told him what we'd heard about Hopgood, especially if Sherlock could be in harm's way. Much as I wanted to move past my affections for Sherlock Holmes, his grasp on me was still quite firm. "He could be in danger?"

"Perhaps. Just let me know if he gets in touch with you, won't you?"

"Of course. Mycroft, I—"

"Yes?"

"Nothing."

He tipped his hat again. "I must be going. I must be about—"

"Her Majesty's business," I said, completing his thought. "Of course."

He stepped around me and waddled toward the Diogenes. Unable to resist, I called out, "Do not over-exert yourself! The fog and physical activity do not well mix!"

He did not answer. He just kept walking.

Before returning to my office, I stopped at the British Museum and went to the room where a beautiful statue of Buddha was displayed. It was a Buddha Vairocana, a Tantric Buddhist image from eastern Java, tenth century. The statue was approximately thirty centimeters high and made of bronze. Buddha's hands were outstretched, like those of a teacher, and represented a form of meditation that vanquishes ignorance. It had played an integral part in the last investigation in which Sherlock and I had been involved.

My mind reeled back to a day I had been in this room, just a little over a year ago, when I met a lovely young man from India named Rabindranath Tagore, who had been studying in England. I had opened up to this stranger, confessed many of my feelings for Sherlock Holmes. He had told me, "Love is an endless mystery." He'd also said, "Weeping is wasted, Miss, on one who does not understand why you cry."

I'd taken his words to heart. I'd tried very hard to stop wasting my tears on Sherlock Holmes. I didn't think that lunch with Jonathan Younger was going to wipe away those tears forever.

But it was a step in the right direction.

12

When I arrived at my office, Penelope Potash was waiting for me. I knew at once that something was very wrong. There was a large welt on her cheek and a cut above her left eye.

I took off my cape and so on and quickly ushered her into the examination room.

"Penelope, what happened?"

"A slight disagreement."

"I would hardly call this slight," I said, gently touching her bruised cheek.

She flinched and said, "It's nothing."

"Was this done by the same man who beat you across your back, Penelope?"

"Can we just do the treatment, please?" she asked as she removed her blouse.

I just stared at her. She coughed and caught her breath. "A client," she finally said.

"A client? What kind of a client would do this to you? Was it the same man who assaulted you? Who beat you?"

She pulled her blouse back together and fastened it. "No," she said, a bit too adamantly. "Nothing to do with that." She paused, looked down and then looked up at me. "What is it you think I do for a living, Dr. Stamford?"

"I do not know, Penelope. You are a cordial, well-mannered, well-dressed young woman. I assumed—"

"A dressmaker perhaps? Or that I work in a milliner's shop? Or some other ladies' shop?"

I nodded, but remembered she'd said she could not avail herself of a privy in a shop because she could not afford to buy anything.

"I walk the streets, Dr. Stamford. I may not look it. I don't wear pink silk stockings or too much rouge. But that's how I put food in my little girl's stomach."

"But you don't act like . . . you certainly don't look like—"

"You think all street women live down on Granby Street and hang out of their windows bare to the waist? Or that we all waltz up and down Haymarket from midnight til morn? I've earned a living that way. I've learned to steal so I could buy my daughter clothes. But I have regular gentlemen callers. Decent blokes. I have some who come on a weekly basis and I get two or three pound a week from each of them. So Mary—that's my daughter—and I can at least afford more than a twelve-foot square room with a bed and a couple chairs and a coal cuttle and a slop pail. I meet the men at a house on James Street. The rooms are clean; there are large beds and a cheval glass. Before I built up a regular clientele, I charged five shillings per customer. Ten per day wasn't all that unusual. It's much better now. My *artistic* name is even in the *Bachelor's Pocket Book*."

"The what?"

She tossed her head back, golden curls falling to her waist as she laughed. "I suppose you never heard of it. It gives bachelors directions to a few houses and describes the women who are available. One of the girls is known as 'Miss Gladiateur,' like the famous French horse who won the English Triple Crown. She wears his colors and advertises that if you mount her, you'll feel like you are galloping atop a thoroughbred. And me—they call me—"

"Penelope," I whispered. "Don't."

"They call me the Mute Swan because I wear a nightdress with sleeves that look like swan wings, and I never say a word. I just do a little graceful dance, entwine and drape and bob and dunk when they ask. I used to watch them, the swans. I used to watch how they move."

She stared at me defiantly but then looked away.

I, too, loved to watch the swans, back in the Broads and here in London, in the river at Victoria Park. Suddenly, my head filled like a poet with a flood of confused, erotic thoughts about love and lovemaking, I remembered how mesmerized I was by them. By how they moved and how they glided across the water, the shiny edges of their delicate feathers glistening in the sunlight. The way they mated always fascinated me. A pair would angle their heads and look at each other and then they would move as one, like an accomplished dancing pair on the floor of a great ballroom. Necks entwined, one bird's neck draped over his partner's, they would caress each other, circling and touching cheek to cheek, moving slowly like white clouds across a violet-blue sky. I'd watch them through to satisfaction, always a little aroused and filled with desire—and envy—myself.

I touched her shoulder. "Penelope, tell me who did this to you. If it is the same man who caused the injuries to your back, he must be stopped. I have friends at the Yard. I—"

She shrugged my hand away. "A man. Just a man."

89

I sat down in front of her and tilted her chin upward. "Penelope. How did you come to have to live like this?"

She tried to look away again but I persisted. "You are not from Cheapside or Covent Garden or Haymarket."

"No, I am not. I was raised in . . . in a nice place. My father was a kind and wonderful man. But he died. And I was not permitted to take his place as I should have been. As I trained all my life to be. And then . . . and then I found myself with child and the man . . . he was very powerful, and very married. He sent me away. He said he was sending me to a safe place. He sent me to a woman in Knightsbridge who ran several brothels. She dressed her ladies well— many of my dresses were costly, made in Paris, and I had jewels. Some real, some not. Most of the good ones I've pawned. But when the baby was born, she tossed us both out, so I found work on the streets. I took lodgings on Dorset for a while. Then on New Street in Bishopsgate. Eventually I was able to make the connection to my present accommodation house. And the chap who runs it—he's good to Mary."

"Oh, Penelope," I whispered, taking her hand.

She smiled weakly. "That's not my real name. I'm Kate. Kate Dew."

"All right. Kate, then. Kate, the first time you came to see me . . . you said that you saw something that you shouldn't. What was it?"

She stood up abruptly. "I've said more than I should. Might you give me some more medicine? For the cough?"

"Of course."

I went to my medicine cabinet and retrieved a small bottle. She outstretched her hand and tried to drop a sovereign into my hand. I folded her fingers over her palms. "Keep it. You and Mary need it more than I."

"I don't want your charity."

"Don't consider it charity then. Consider it payment for an enlightening, educational afternoon. After all, prior to today, I knew nothing of the *Bachelor's Pocket Book*."

She actually giggled at that but she still slipped the sovereign into my pocket.

I was about to hand it to her when one of Sherlock's young errand boys came rushing into the office.

"Miss! 'ere. A message from Mr. 'olmes."

I recognized the boy; his name was Rattle and he was about eight or nine years of age. Still thin as a scarecrow, still wearing overalls and a frayed cap above his black, sleek hair, he always remnded me of a street sweeper. "One moment, Rattle," I cautioned. "I am with a patient."

I gave the bottle to Kate and said, "I'll see you next week, Kate."

She nodded and left.

As I took the message from Rattle, a thought split through my brain like lighting rupturing the sky. I stopped and stared into space.

They call her the mute swan, I thought. In that despicable, deplorable bachelor's guide to women of the night. Her father had died, leaving her penniless. Her father, she'd said earlier, had had to make a living by cleaning urinals at St. James Palace for four shillings a week when he could not do his regular job.

The boy Sherlock had spoken to, Thomas Abnett, told him that a Deputy Swankeeper had died, but his son stayed on for a while and then disappeared. Abnett said he was very distressed that is father was treated shabbily. And there was something else. What was it? *Yes,* I thought, *I remember.* Something to do with a member of Privy Council and the boy.

Kate had told me that she had trained all her life to fill her father's shoes in his occupation. But she was not permitted to take his place. Why? Why couldn't she? Because she was a girl, not a boy? Because her gender was discovered when this married man, her lover, made her pregnant and sent her away?

'They call me the Mute Swan because I wear a nightdress with sleeves that look like swan wings,' she'd said.

What if Kate knew all about swans, had been trained by her father to become a swan keeper, but could not occupy such a position because she was a girl? What if she and her father had hidden that fact from everyone but then, with her pregnancy, she was turned out on the streets by the Queen?

"Rattle!" I shouted. "Rattle, I have a job for you," I said as I knelt down and placed my hands on his shoulders. "That young woman who just left. The pretty one wearing the blue dress. You saw her, didn't you?"

He nodded.

I reached into my pocket and held the sovereign out to him. "This is yours. Follow her. Follow her and then come back and tell me *exactly* where she lives. Now she may go to James Street or she may go to New Street in Bishopsgate."

"Worlds apart, Miss."

"I know. But I must know both addresses. Another half-crown to you if come back here with both addresses."

"But the message from Mr. 'olmes . . . ."

"Yes, yes, give it to me. Now hurry so you do not lose sight of the woman. And do not let her know you are following her, Rattle."

"Me, Miss? Rattle is like a shadow."

He quickly turned and dashed down the hall.

"Run," I whispered. "Run, run, little shadow."

13

Sherlock's message was cryptic, as usual. "Currently out of the Metropolis. Expect to have much information beyond the obvious facts when I return. Should be back tomorrow evening. Meet me at Four Swans Inn, Bishopsgate at seven."

"Bishopsgate," I said to myself.

Bishopsgate was named after one of the original eight gates, in the London Wall. It was one of the main entrances to the city built by the Romans to defend their strategically important port town on the River Thames, Londinium. Many old coaching inns that accommodated passengers setting out on the Old North Road were there . . . the Old Bull Inn, the Flower Pot, the White Hart. It was thought that some of these inns were built on cellars constructed by the Romans. Until the railway lines out of Liverpool Street had opened a few years before, the inns were always busy with passengers and goods transported by wagon. Even now, many men leaving their offices for home would stop at one of these taverns after work. Despite the decrease in coaching passengers, they did a good bar trade.

Swans dominated the motif on Bishopsgate and Gracechurch Streets. At the south end of Gracechurch was the Four Swans. To the north, was the One Swan, and not far from there was Two Swans Inn. I'd been to the Four Swans only once with Uncle Ormond when London Hospital was short-staffed and desperate enough to allow even a woman doctor to lend a hand. I remembered the rump steak and kidney pudding and the balcony above the courtyard with its beautiful depiction of four stately swans.

I thought of the mutilated swans and Kate Dew's "artistic name." Had Sherlock discovered a link between her and the swan investigation as well?

I tended to several more patients, all the while thinking about Kate and what Sherlock was up to. I gave thought to contacting Mycroft to tell him of Sherlock's whereabouts but I didn't really know them. I knew only that, for whatever reason, he wasn't in London. I was about to close up my office when Rattle returned, out of breath, panting, as always.

"Miss, I'm back."

"I see that Rattle. What did you find out?"

"The lady . . . she went to a place on James Street. Stayed on an 'our. Jus' 'bout. Then t' New Street. Buller's 'ouse."

"Is it a workhouse?"

He shook his head. "More a dosshouse, Miss. 'Cross from th' Bishopsgate police station."

"Cheap lodging then."

He nodded. "Wiggins knows th'owner. Will'm Buller and 'is wife Eliza. Moved from St. Giles."

He went on to say that the house was not far from some warehouses owned by St. Katherine's Dock Company and the East India Depot, and a fire station. It was close to the Liverpool Railway Station . . . and not far from Spitalfields. I was sure Wiggins knew the area well. Despite the traffic to the taverns, the East End was not the most hospitable portion of London. If I met Sherlock there, I might just take young Wiggins with me.

95

14

I picked at dinner that night. I was not hungry for one thing. Secondly, Aunt Susan had hired a new cook and she wasn't very good. After Martha, the previous cook, was fired for having let Sherlock into the house without consent, Aunt Susan hurriedly looked for someone else. Sherlock had persuaded Martha to give him a key to the servants' door to let himself in as part of an elaborate ruse to catch out the British Museum murderer. She was tangled in one of Sherlock's spidery webs and, ultimately, his plan had served to free my uncle from gaol and send the real killer to the gallows. But no amount of persuasion on his part, nor mine, would dissuade Aunt Susan from terminating Martha. The servants were permitted no visitors without permission; certainly no one was allowed to have a key to the house, not even Sherlock Holmes.

I stayed up long after Aunt Susan retired to wait for my uncle. I lit a fire, gathered an array of gas lamps, sipped port, and passed the time reading Effie's journal, the one she had entrusted to her cousin Oscar Wilde to give to me when he saw fit. He'd done so a year after she passed away giving birth to my nephew. I had never been able to read all of it. I read it in fits and starts because so often the memories pressing into my heart were as painful as a bird savagely pierced against a long, sharp thorn. I turned now to an entry in what she called the *Last Diary of Euphemia O'Flahertie Stamford*. She'd made it early in her pregnancy.

6 October 1876

   "I am puzzled—and frightened—by a dream I had last night. I was wading in the river . . . in Victoria Park, I believe. I was encircled by swans. So beautiful. White like those we would find in the shady woodlands and hedgerows near your parents' home. They reminded me of enchanted nightshade—you know the ones with the little white flowers and the soft, downy feathers. Their wings were like that.

   "Then, all at once, the swans surrounded me; their wings flapped violently and then they pounced upon me and one began biting me from the base of my neck to further down my spine. Savagely pushing me down further and further into the water though I tried desperately to get to the shore. Down, down. And suddenly my head went beneath the water. I would rise, gasp, make a mewing sound as the swan pushed me back down, beating me with its wings. But then another swan came, challenging my attacker. She was almost airborne as she attacked my assailant full from the rear, biting and beating him with her wings. Again and again with feet and wings and bill. I realized it was you, you who was

saving me, circling around and around me to
protect me like a warrior-maiden.

"*But it was too late. I went limp and*
sunk down, deep, deep into the dark water. I
saw faces. Hundreds of faces and dead eyes. No
bodies, Poppy. Just heads, bodiless heads,
bobbing about.

"*I don't know what it means.*"

I shut the journal. Often Effie's dreams manifested themselves in some kind of terrible and real event. Obviously, she had, in her own strange way, foreseen my involvement with the swan case that we were investigating. But there was more to it than that. These heads, these faces . . . I could not help but wonder if the swans were in some way connected to this dismembered body Wiggins had dug up.

It was close to midnight when Uncle came home. I heard him come in, latch the door, and call out to Aunt Susan. I shouted to him and he came to the library door. Though he was now in his early fifties, Uncle was still a very handsome man. He was athletic, fair-haired, but now sported a grizzled moustache and beard. Like Sherlock, Uncle had curious ways and eerie tricks of spotting details that others missed.

"Uncle Ormond, you're very late. Aunt Susan is asleep."

"He sighed. Very busy day. And night. A young woman came into the hospital just as I was leaving. She had tried to abort her child. She botched it and the uterus prolapsed. I was unable to save her."

"I'm so sorry. Are you alright?"

"I am a surgeon. I suppose I should be used to it by now. But one never gets used to it. So, may I join you?"

"Of course." I rose, poured some port into a glass and handed it to him. We sat down in the wing chairs that flanked the fireplace.

He swirled the wine so hard it almost splashed out of his glass. "I ran into two young men of your acquaintance today."

"Who might they be?" I asked, knowing full well the answer.

"Sherlock, who at my friend Mycroft's request is still investigating the swan case, and who is, to Mycroft's consternation, in full pursuit of facts surrounding that poor fellow who young Wiggins disinterred."

"Why does Mycroft wish him to stay out of the case, Uncle?"

"Because it could be quite dangerous. It's for the Yard to sort out."

"I also ran into Mycroft today. He said the man was a member of the Privy Council."

"Yes, his identity is now known," Uncle said. "I'm sure it will be in all the papers tomorrow. He has something to do with the Board of Trade at Whitehall Gardens. In the Railway Department, I believe. His name was Cecil Gray."

"And what else is known about him?"

"Very little. He is—was—married. Had a daughter who died very recently. In fact, it was in her grave that Wiggins found the body."

"His daughter's grave? My God."

"Yes, terrible circumstances."

"Has he anything to do with Oxford? Was he interested in phrenology?"

Uncle cocked his head. "What makes you ask?"

"If you spoke to Sherlock, then you must know that we suspect that someone was funding an Oxford professor's research in that regard. Wiggins was sending bodies by rail to Oxford. So I must wonder—"

"Stop wondering, Poppy," Uncle said in a stern voice. "You—and Sherlock—must let the Yard handle this."

"Sometimes they are out of their depth."

"You parrot Sherlock."

"Perhaps he is right. You should know that first hand."

He knew I was referring to the British Museum murders Sherlock had solved the previous year, the false accusations against Uncle which were part of a ruse concocted by Mycroft to flush out the true criminal. It had nearly ended very badly.

"The second young man I spoke with today was Jonathan Younger," he said to change the subject.

"Yes, I ran into him today also."

"He wanted to know if he could take you to dinner tomorrow night."

"Dinner? No, I told him perhaps lunch. Actually I have plans with Sherlock tomorrow evening."

"You are not still pining for Sherlock, are you, Poppy?"

I felt my face flush and momentarily turned away. Then I faced him squarely. "Pining," I sneered. "I do not pine."

"Hanging on to a scrap of hope then?"

I looked down, into my glass, and swirled the crimson liquid myself this time. I looked back at Uncle and asked, "Do you remember the young man I told you about, the poet I met at the British Museum? The one from India?"

He nodded.

"He told me once that a mind all logic is like a knife all blade. It makes the hand bleed that uses it. I have come to agree with him."

"I see," he said, but his eyes betrayed his skepticism. "So then . . . Jonathan Younger."

"What about him?"

He smiled. "I told him that I place no restrictions on my very intelligent, educated, logical, independent, willful niece."

I laughed. "I take after my uncle."

"And so he would like to take you to lunch tomorrow at noon at The Criterion. I suggested the Holburn. Aunt Susan and I were there the other night for dinner. We had fish, sweets, ices and cheese—wonderful bread, as well. All for three shillings and six pence. Quite good."

"Did you tell Jonathan that I would meet him there?"

"I advised him to send a page to confirm all this. And I told him that if you had not arrived by half twelve, he'd best have something to eat by himself or go back to Bart's hungry."

"All right then," I said with a smile.

He finished his port and said, "I'm going to get some sleep. You should, too."

He started to rise but I reached out to touch his elbow. "Uncle."

"Yes?"

"I heard something . . . I heard something quite despicable about St. Bart's today."

He settled back into the chair. "What was that?"

"Sherlock said that they used to . . . well, he told me that at a public house there was a room in the back with benches with the grave robbers' names who waited there with specimens for the surgeons at St. Bart's to appraise and purchase."

His face fell. "The Fortune of War public house on Pie Corner. Yes, Sherlock is correct."

"It's true then," I said, heaving a loud breath. "And so, despite acts of Parliament and the Poor Laws, grave robbing still occurs."

"Yes, it does, because there has been such an influx of medical students that there are not enough bodies for dissection. This has to do with this Wiggins thing, doesn't it, Poppy?"

"Yes."

"Poppy, I urge you not to—"

I interrupted him mid-sentence. "Uncle, in a very twisted way, I do see why the purchase of cadavers, this black market is on-going."

"Oxford is still a somewhat marginalized medical school, Poppy. A lot of the metropolitan medical schools at the hospitals are booming. And we don't get enough bodies to meet the needs of the medical students. So we still resort to finding beggars, and homeless and prostitutes and poor people who are willing to contract away their dying relatives. Brokers, undertakers, and others still pay the poor to give up their dead or simply help themselves and lie to relatives who want to at least give the deceased a pauper's funeral. Still, to this day, body-dealers and those who specialize in body parts pick up corpses and sell them for profit . . . for a sixpence or a few shillings. The price of a meal at the Holburn," he choked.

"And they are transported to various places on the railway?"

"On what they call dead trains."

"My God. Uncle, this is—"

"Despicable. Nothing of which the medical profession can be proud. There are those who fight for the poor and unsuspecting. People like Hussey in Oxford."

"Hussey? I thought he was something of a dolt."

"Do not believe everything you hear, Poppy. He trained at St. Bart's. He is the coroner in Oxford now, elected by the town council a couple of years ago. He has refused to provide any unclaimed bodies to Radcliffe Infirmary and he has lobbied against guardians selling the

103

bodies of the poor for dissection. He constantly wages a war against people selling their loved ones.

"Poppy, there are dealers who employ go-betweens, like porters at hospitals and workhouse masters and undertakers. Of course, young medical students must learn all they can about the human body, but this trafficking of bodies and body parts . . . . "

His voice trailed off. I simply nodded. It was exactly what Sherlock had been telling me earlier.

"Poppy, I don't know what kind of scheme young Wiggins involved himself in. I don't know if this Cecil Gray he dug up has anything to do with this at all. But stay out of it, will you? Promise me?"

Uncle had asked me this before. His concern for me was always at odds with what Sherlock asked this of me. He had frequently cautioned me to check my feelings for Sherlock and to disentangle myself from Sherlock's detective pursuits. But it was a tug-of-war—complying with Uncle's caring requests or submitting to Sherlock's urgent entreaties.

Uncle always lost.

15

I lay in bed for a long time, unable to sleep, thinking about the sordid business of body snatching. Obviously, the Anatomy Act had done nothing to better or cheapen medical training. There was a shortage of bodies and teaching hospitals with a focus on dissection needs must equal corpses being provided somehow . . . by mortuaries or workhouses or gaols. And if that wasn't enough . . . and if coroners like the wrongly reputed Hussey, however well-intentioned he might be, stepped in to thwart relatives from selling bodies and refused to let every corpse that came through the Radcliffe Infirmary be carted off prematurely, then this illegal trade would continue.

Oxford had remained a limited provincial medical school, particularly in development of clinical medicine. So bodies were even more sorely needed. And so, this Professor, this Danford Hopgood would have all the more difficult time obtaining corpses for his 'research.' I needed to talk to Wiggins. I needed to ask him to accompany me to meet Sherlock and I wanted to find out everything he knew about this degenerate, repugnant trade.

The following morning, a page called upon us during breakfast with a message from Jonathan that he would send a carriage for me to take me to The Criterion for our luncheon. I asked the page to relate to Jonathan that I needed no carriage; I would walk.

After he left, I set out for St. Paul's where I so often went to contemplate things. If I desired a chaperone on my trek to the Four Swans and if I wanted to speak with Wiggins, first I had to find him. How did Sherlock contact him? Logical as I thought myself to be, it was worth trying to dissect Sherlock's methods.

I arrived at the cathedral around ten. How often I had come here to pray for guidance or to ask that the burden of my affection for Sherlock Holmes be lifted.

As always, I marvelled at St. Paul's exterior, taking in her extreme beauty . . . a mighty temple of colossal proportions, especially the front view at Ludgate Bill. The façade, a pediment, was sustained by a double colonnade and flanked by two towers. Once there had been Paul's Cross where people preached sermons and politics mixed with religion in a way that had mostly passed. Now a statue of Queen Anne stood where the cross once was.

I entered the door to the left of the northern portico. Only once had I ascended to the top of the dome so I could look down on the nave and the transept, the fresco with depictions of the life of the patron saint. Looking down from the grandeur of the dome, I had often wondered how these works could be accomplished from that dizzying height. A light gallery encircles the top of the dome some five hundred steps upward, and from there one could see all of London, its great avenues, its patches of green, the river winding its way and the bridges spanning it with steamers and wherries and sailing vessels making their way to where I always wondered. My feelings were always strangely mingled. Sometimes I longed to leave England, to immerse myself in other cultures, to venture, as Victor had, to a far off place like India. But if I did, would I miss my relatives? Would I miss my parents, Uncle Ormond and Aunt Susan? This church? Would I long to still be wandering the streets with Sherlock—Farrington and Holburn, Oxford? And Fleet, the bustling lane of the offices of *Punch* and *The Standard* and *The Daily Telegraph*?

I sat down in a pew and closed my eyes. I forced myself to retrace the many moments when I sat quietly spellbound, listening to Sherlock. He knew he was special and was immodest about the fact. He'd once said that no one would ever bring to a case the amount of study and talent that he would. I believed it was in part due to the fact that he played the game for the game's sake, rather than out of any deep concern for society. He was not totally deficient in human sympathy but oh, there were times when he seemed to be. He loved to push beyond the mundane, to put himself in peril if need be to pursue his goal—defeating criminals, solving the crimes. The thrill of the chase was as important, perhaps more exciting, than ultimately solving it. He could be like a racehorse, driven round the track, nostrils flaring, heart thumping, hooves thundering, absolutely and single-mindedly focused on the matter at hand. For him that was solving the unsolvable, to the point of deafness and blindness to everything else. If anything disturbed Sherlock, it was the possibility that a clue might have slipped by him or been dismissed as unimportant. He had told me repeatedly to discard distraction from my life, including romantic notions as he had worked so hard to do, and yet he kept his mind open to extraordinary possibilities, to look at a problem from many different angles.

He had asked me once, when we were sitting by the river during his holiday at Victor Trevor's home, "Mary's father has three daughters. The oldest is named April. The next oldest is May. The youngest is named what?"

I had been reading and occasionally watching the white clouds slowly snake their way across the bluest of skies. I mumbled 'June."

He had laughed. "You are not paying attention. Though you are trying to think in a logical way, you are not really listening. Mary is one of three daughters. Her sisters are April and May. The third must be, therefore, named Mary."

I believe I'd thrown my book at him.

Though he was arrogant enough that he rarely admitted a mistake, he counselled that we must all learn from our mistakes and those of others. He would forgive one mistake but certainly no more than that.

He never guessed. He accumulated evidence and data. He asked the right questions. He evaluated and formed a hypothesis and then reached a conclusion. He constantly worked on improving his inductive skills.

After a time, resolved that dissecting Sherlock's brain—what little I knew of it—would not lead me to Wiggins or Rattle or Ollie or Scratch or any of Sherlock's other young cohorts, I sighed, stood up and muttered to myself, "This is getting me nowhere." None of the things I'd learned from Sherlock were going to help me find one homeless boy in a city of thousands.

As I emerged, I saw a young girl, perhaps twelve or thirteen years of age, with loose, dirty brown curls and eyes like an owl's. She wore a long, grey tattered skirt and a shortgown, something one would expect to see on a washerwoman decades ago. It was T-shaped with a flared hem, the kind of garment that might be suitable for physical labor. It was made of corded linen, and was long ago off-white but now discolored with age that was more obvious against her pasty skin. It had been patched many times, especially along the sleeves and beneath the arms, with the tiny stitches of a skilled and frugal hand. Her battered boots were dusty. She walked up to me and said, "I'm 'ere t'say Wiggins'll fetch yer 'round six to take yer to Sherlock."

"What? Who are you?"

"Ivy. Ivy Green."

"Well, Ivy, how did you find me?"

"Wiggins says that Mr. 'olmes says you come 'ere sometimes to think. So's I followed and waited fer yer t' be done prayin'."

"Wiggins said that, did he?"

She nodded.

"And you'll go back to Master Wiggins to confirm that you found me then."

She nodded again.

"And what will you get for your trouble?"

Now she shrugged and said, "Maybe a shilling. Mr. 'olmes will see to it."

Laughing, I gave her a shilling from my pocket and said, "You deserve this and more. Do tell Archie—I mean, Wiggins, I look forward to seeing him then. At my home?"

Again, Ivy nodded.

"All right then. Thank you, Ivy."

Wide-eyed, she said, "That's a fine scarf, Miss. And your cape . . . ."

"Ivy, why don't you come with Wiggins tonight and we'll give you a decent supper?"

I wanted to take her straightaway to a shop to buy her clothing as well, but she fidgeted as if she could not wait to get on with her day. "No, Miss. I'll be off then."

Before I could object, she turned and ran up Fleet Street.

Well, so much for comprehending Sherlock Holmes or any of his little friends, I thought.

16

I walked down Regent Street toward Piccadilly Circus where I was to meet Jonathan at The Criterion Theater and Restaurant. Built on what had once been the site of a coaching inn called the White Bear, it had thrived for over a century but was demolished in 1870 and rebuilt. I was just fourteen and my uncle and I watched from a distance. He had squeezed my hand and said, "We must never forget the past, Poppy, what's gone before. It is alive in the present if we keep it so."

Ground for the new building was broken in 1871; a restaurant and a bar opened in 1873 and the theater presented its first performance, *An American Lady*, in 1874, the year I met Sherlock. I stood at the entrance for a moment. Many, many years later, I would revisit that site where a statue, Eros, was erected a few years after that luncheon, which I came to regard as the real turning point in my life. Ultimately the decision to meet Jonathan that day set into motion a series of events that altered the course of my existence.

I spotted Jonathan and when he saw me enter the restaurant, he gallantly rushed to escort me to our table, took my cape and handed it to a waiter as he held my chair out for me to be seated.

It was a lovely setting with clean linen tablecloths, neatly pressed napkins, plated silverware, pewter pots and finger glasses. We were immediately offered a choice of cheeses and pulled bread. A waiter handed me a bill-of-fare but Jonathan quickly suggested flounder and potatoes and I simply nodded.

"We can order something else, if you prefer, Poppy."

"No Jonathan. Flounder is fine."

"My father," he said, "often likes to tell me about all the restaurants he and my mother frequented when he was a young solicitor before he became an MP in Suffolk. I believe his favorite place was George Reeves on Cornhill and Lombard. He used to rave about the roast beef and mutton cutlets and hashed duck and new potatoes."

We sat there, me rather stiff and uncomfortable as Jonathan rapidly recounted his days at Harrow with my brother Michael and his struggle to decide whether to follow his father's footsteps into the law or to pursue medicine.

On this subject, medicine, we found common ground and conversation eased through the rest of lunch . . . until he asked me this: "What is the nature of your relationship with Sherlock Holmes? Why do you keep company with him?"

I dabbed my lips with my napkin, took a sip of water and said, "Pardon me?"

"I asked what your relationship to him is."

My mind flitted from one memory to another, from the day I met Sherlock on the grounds of Oxford to our long afternoons by the river in the Broads when he visited Victor Trevor, to his disappearance to sort out a blackmail scheme against Victor's father. He'd summoned me to Holme-Next-the-Sea to seek my counsel as to how to tell Victor about his father's sordid past from which Mrs. Hudson's estranged husband's blackmail scheme was hatched. It was at that seaside cottage that we had finally displayed our affection toward one another. I thought of the criminal cases we had worked together. I often placed myself in danger to do so. I thought of our meetings at the British Museum where he researched certain Buddhist practices as they related to our last case. I saw in my mind his lodgings on Montague, which I had seen only once. The roaring fireplace, the mantel where he kept notes and pipes. And the tavern at which he often stopped, the one across the street from the museum. There were many public houses but this was his favorite and I pictured him sitting in there, nursing a beer and thinking through a problem.

Finally, I thought of the way my feelings waxed and waned toward Sherlock.

"Poppy?" Jonathan asked, snapping me back to the present. "I do not mean to offend but I have wondered . . . ."

"Sherlock is my very dear friend, Jonathan. We have known each other a long time and worked together on many cases."

"Cases? You? But you are not a detective."

"I lend my medical expertise occasionally. And I assist in other ways."

"So it is a business relationship."

"No, we are friends," I said again. "Why does this matter to you?"

"Michael has told me a great deal about Sherlock Holmes. I think he is . . . well, he is not suitable for you."

I smiled to myself. Then I laughed.

"What's so funny?"

"That is almost precisely what Sherlock said to me about you."

"He doesn't even know me," he protested. "What makes him think that I am unsuitable for you?"

"Jonathan, it really does not matter to me what either one of you think. I go my own way and I shall make my own decisions. Men—even ones for whom I have affection—do not make them for me."

Now Jonathan laughed. "I knew you were different, Poppy. Independent. As I told you, I find it exciting. I should like to see you again."

I glanced at the watch pinned to my bodice. "I must be going, Jonathan," I said as I stood and waved to a waiter to retrieve my cape.

Jonathan stood and said, "Poppy, let me hail you a cab or—"

"No, thank you, Jonathan. As I told your page earlier, I prefer to walk."

As soon as I had my cape, I drew it around me, tied it, thanked him for lunch and headed back to my office.

Men, I thought. Men! Is there not a single man in the world who would allow a woman to be—well, whatever she wishes?

17

The day passed slowly, despite another flurry of patients. I counted the hours until Wiggins would escort me to The Four Swans to consult with Sherlock about the two cases—the dead swans and the dead Privy Council member.

Despite Uncle's protest, I sat near the front door to wait with cape, scarf and bonnet on. As the grandfather clock struck six, I jumped. Just moments later, Wiggins knocked on the door and I raced to open it.

"There's a hansom waiting t' take us on t' th' Four Swans, Miss," he said.

"Let us go then, Archie. I mean, Wiggins," I said, grabbing my gloves and hooking my arm through his.

It seemed to take forever to get to the East End and all the longer because each time I tried to query Wiggins about his grave robbing enterprise, he either refused to answer or simply looked away. The Four Swans was in sight when Wiggins signaled the cabbie to stop. As we exited the hansom, I felt the squalor. All around me—the stench of sewers and drains, the foul odour of sweaty people molded to one another in the cheap lodgings, the pall of hopelessness washed down by pale ale. There was no hint that anyone in this desolate area would reap the harvest of their labors or aspirations. They had stopped dreaming long ago.

Before I took two steps, Sherlock emerged from the shadows. "Follow me," he said gruffly. So began a sojourn down Commercial Street between Flower and Dean and Aldgate, near Whitechapel. "What are we doing, Sherlock? Where are we going?"

"Quiet, Poppy," he said, gently taking me by the elbow to prod me along. "We will return to the Four Swans soon to have a meal and I will give you an account of our case."

"Which case? The mutilated swans or the dismembered corpse?"

"Both. But first, do come along and observe."

"But where are we going, Sherlock?"

"Just follow me."

We finally stopped in an alley near Court Street directly across from London Hospital. Sherlock pointed to a woman standing beneath a gas lamp near a doorway several yards away. She was small in stature, with long brown hair and wore a crimson dress and a black bonnet trimmed with a wine-colored ribbon.

Many other women paraded along Commercial, most dressed neatly, hawking trinkets and menthol cones or in search of clients. I knew their lives likely alternated from lodging houses to workhouses to the pavement.

"Sherlock," I whispered, but he put finger to lips and said, "Quiet. Observe."

The woman looked back and forth as if she were waiting for someone.

"Sherlock, you must tell me at once what we are doing here or—"

"Ssshh," he cautioned.

A few moments later, a man came from Thomas Street to her left. She turned and raised her skirts above her ankles. He spoke to her, then cupped her face with his hands. They turned to cross Court Street and he paused to fondle her beneath another gas lamp. It was then that I was able to focus on his face.

I realized it was Jonathan Younger.

18

Soon they were laughing and groping each other like fecund feral cats. The woman emitted a series of unrelenting groans as Jonathan explored her, right there on the street. Then they stepped into a rowhouse and shut the door behind them.

It is difficult to describe the feelings I experienced in that moment. I had no deep affection for Jonathan. We were not in a significant relationship. Yet I felt a sense of betrayal. He was my brother's dear friend. I'd agreed to be with him in a social setting and I had hoped that perhaps a new relationship would help me push away any romantic feelings I still nurtured for Sherlock. Whether I acquiesced to Jonathan's pursuit was immaterial. It would have meant I was reasserting my emotional independence, that I was willing to discard Sherlock from my life entirely.

I closed my eyes for a moment, willing my surroundings to disappear, willing the clattering of horses and hansoms that heaped this reality upon me to vanish into the fog. My mind went to the Broads, to the river where some beautiful creature is always going about its business. I was sitting on the grass, watching birds float above, flailing their wings . . . teal and wigeon, reed and sedge warblers. I watched a marsh harrier career at full tilt, clapping its wings, stalling above a rock and then banking off across the river. And then the butterflies floated by, mute, graceful, leading a short life of pure innocence. Swallowtails or a rare Norfolk hawker dragonfly, turning at this angle and that on the wind, shadowing the sunlight, nesting on a fen orchid or a crested buckler fern, then taking flight once more and waving goodbye as it disappears into a chink.

Come, a voice said to me. Come home and be greeted by your friends back home. Walk along the river, navigate the patchwork of waterways, watch for the harvest mice and water shrews and listen, listen to the swans gliding along the water.

But no. Reality is fixed, demanding. I could feel the roar of it, rough and grating inside my head like the rumble of a mile-high wave seething and heaving and crashing against the rocks. Even if you leave momentarily, it always follows, it always calls you back.

"Poppy," Sherlock said and I turned to look at him. "You see who it is."

The color draining from my face, I nodded. I felt water drip on the back of my neck as snow heaved off the muzzle of fog and broke through.

Go back to the Broads, my mind told me. Skip along the water's edge. Let it roll down and slide along the top of your foot. Dip your toes in and cast a long glance back to London and laugh at her. You are not supposed to be there, you are supposed to be here with us, the creatures called.

"Poppy, I spoke with Womack yesterday. I inquired as to Jonathan. He is the one who told me of his almost nightly visits to avail himself of . . . of this. A friend of Jonathan's who works at London Hospital has introduced him to many of these . . . women. I spoke to Womack about the house where Dr. Younger meets his . . . his—"

I spit out, "Stop!" and Wiggins walked a few paces away as if to hide from this unusual spat between two people he admired. I longed for Sherlock's face to slip away as well, out of the glare of the light. I longed for darkness to surround me, soft and restful, for the light to desert me for as long as I willed it.

I tried to think of something clever. Instead I blurted, "You are cruel, Sherlock. You . . . you do not want me yourself but you don't want anyone else to want me either."

"It would be a pity if you truly believed that, Poppy. You may not like the message but I am simply the messenger," he said softly. "Sometimes the very thing you wish least to hear is that which you need most to hear. And, in this case, to see, because I do not think you would have listened to me if you did not see it for yourself."

In the deepest levels of my soul, I knew he was right. Still, I was angry. And there awakened in me an anguish that would later emigrate to resolve and become forever inseparable from it. That resolve would be indissolubly united with all the pain that loving Sherlock had caused me. I determined that I would never give into my emotions so completely again.

"I should like to leave now, Sherlock."

"We have things to discuss. I have a lead on the killer. And possibly a connection to the person who is destroying the swans."

"I do not care." I walked away briskly and Wiggins raced up to me.

"But, Miss, yer was wantin' me t' talk about the grave diggin'."

I saw a hansom coming toward me, stepped into the roadway and waved to it. It stopped. "Not now. I will talk to you . . . another time."

"But, Poppy," Sherlock said.

As I stepped up into the cab, Sherlock took my wrist and borrowed a little fragment from the truth. "Forgive me," he said. "I was trying to be helpful."

I knew he wanted to show me he was right about Jonathan after all. In fact, he probably wanted to show me how senseless and illogical it was to be in a romantic relationship. But he may also have been sorry to hurt me.

"And you have been. Very helpful indeed."

I had chosen. My fate was settled. I would fend off lofty romantic notions that might pull at my soul; I would allow them no longer to get in my way. In separating from Sherlock, I needed to be like him. Cold, disentangled from love and emotion, oblivious to the incessant stream of images from our night together.

As the cab pulled away, I heard him call out my name. I did not look back.

19

The cab bumped along and my mind sputtered and spun, but as I, too, tended toward the science of deduction, the logical course of things, I summarily dismissed Jonathan as a non-entity. I quickly decided that he did not matter. His sordid night life did not matter. I would at the proper time relate this evening's revelations to my dear brother who thought of Jonathan as a friend—he needed to know the sort of man he was befriending. But right now, Jonathan's lifestyle, his existence was insignificant.

In my mind, just as in Sherlock's, what mattered at this instance was *the case*. I did not have all the facts and that is what I needed. I knew that Kate had had a loving father but after he died, her life went to hell. I knew that she'd ended up a prostitute to support the child her married lover had fathered. I sensed her affinity to swans and from her comments, I sensed that she detested the fact that she was a woman in a man's world, that she respected me for having forged my way through the barriers. I knew that she had seen something that resulted in a terrible beating. A warning to keep her silent. If all this was connected to the boy who had disappeared from the Queen's employ and the rumours about the member of the Privy Council, if it was related to the dead Cecil Gray, I certainly could not prove that yet.

But as we trotted along, as London's filth spewed around us, as loquacious beggars ran beside the cab and pawnbrokers and dealers hawked their wares, as the rambling residents of London's underworld and the shrill sounds of her desperate characters propelled like shooting stars through the night, I realized that this was exactly where I needed to be and Sherlock was exactly who I needed to speak to.

To him and to Kate Dew. Wiggins would know exactly where to find her. Rattle had given me the addresses after he followed her and Wiggins knew the area.

I shouted to the cabbie to turn around. He made a turn so sharp that I thought I would cascade from the cab as we headed back from whence we came. Along the way, more ladies of the evening appeared, some lady-like in appearance who had obviously used taste in selecting their clothing. A few were dressed in bright colors, their dresses meretricious and tawdry. A stout woman on the corner of Thomas with a round face and thick, muscular arms was talking to a man of equal girth, quite obviously negotiating a price. I signaled the cabbie to stop and tossed him several coins as I emerged from the cab. I ran to where I'd left Sherlock and Wiggins and nearly collided with them as they rounded the corner.

"Poppy!" Sherlock cried. "You . . . what on earth are you . . . ?"

"Be quiet," I said. "We need to talk."

"Poppy, I am sorry, truly but—"

"Still your tongue, will you? I have need of a glass of wine and you must listen to me."

We went to the Four Swans and Sherlock ordered beverages, some cold meats and cheese. I proceeded to tell

123

Sherlock about Kate Dew. I related what she had said about her father and his demotion to cleaning urinals at St. James, about being unable to follow his footsteps in his unnamed profession, about her relationship with a married man which resulted in the illicit birth of her daughter, and her preoccupation with swans and her disdain for the queen. He sat, wide-eyed, taking it all in, his mind like a Babbage calculating machine tying all the loose ends together. Then he leaned forward. "Dew? You said her surname was Dew?"

I nodded.

"Poppy, you remember I told you that I could not speak to the Keeper of the Swans as he was ill? He finally recovered from his bronchial infection and he was able to speak to me."

"And?"

"And he told me more about swans than I have an interest in but also gave me some useful information. A man named Charles Dew was a Deputy Keeper of the Swans for many, many years. He had a son who would be in his twenties now. At least it was thought it was a son."

I felt my eyebrows rise. "Thought?"

"The assistant keeper was injured and could not complete his daily duties. He was demoted to maintaining urinals at St. James. Just as your patient described about her father. The Keeper went into great detail about those as well. How glazed stoneware basins and marble divisions replaced the iron and slate and that now metal perforated with geometric patterns—"

"Sherlock," I interrupted, impatient to hear the real story.

"The son stayed on for awhile, helping with the swans, but apparently rumours started to fly about some unusual relationship with a member of the Privy Council. At first, so the Keeper thought, the gentleman of high birth had simply taken an interest in the boy who apparently was quite bright. But then people started to talk about it being something more. And the Keeper has come to believe that those rumours were wrong, too.

"He went to great length to explain how many young women in America's Civil War dressed as men to join the war effort. He said that he and Mr. Dew had discussed this on many occasions."

"The Civil War ended over a decade ago."

"Indeed, round about the time the man started to work with the swans and started bringing his son with him. The Keeper has come to the conclusion that the man's son was not a boy at all but a female and that the Privy Council member eventually became involved with the girl. That is why she left."

"And the Privy Council member . . . who was it?"

"Our dismembered corpse, Dr. Stamford. Cecil Gray."

"So now," I said, leaning toward him, "if we pull all of this together . . . Kate's account of her life, what she told me about her father, her illegitimate child, the fact that Cecil Gray was involved with Mr. Dew's alleged son . . . ."I sat back, took a sip of wine, left that string of facts hanging for a moment and then looked straight at Wiggins.

"Wha'?" he asked.

"Do you think your commission came from Mr. Gray?"

He shook his head. "I don' know. No idea."

I told him the address to Kate's lodgings and asked, "Can you show us the way?"

He nodded.

"Take us there, Wiggins."

He shrugged and stood. "Awright, Miss."

20

"Sherlock," I said, "You told me that you had a lead on Sir Gray's case."

"Hopkins told me that Hopgood, the professor at Oxford, disappeared around the same time as Cecil Gray. I went to Oxford. No one knows where he went."

"I see," I whispered.

When we arrived at the lodgings of Kate Dew, another young woman greeted us at the door with a toddler in her arms. We asked for Kate and the woman directed us to a lodging house around the corner. She said Kate was an excellent cook and that she was fixing a meal for a sick friend.

We hurried there; in fact, Sherlock's long stride was so quick that Wiggins and I could barely keep up. When we found the windowless cellar house, we knocked on the door and the woman who answered looked gaunt and sickly. We asked for Kate and received a half-hearted response and a wave toward the stove. It was not like some lodgings I'd heard about. No rats swarmed the floor, no meagre rations of water were passed around. There was a stove for heat and cooking, the floor was covered with a colorful rug, the dinner table had a cloth and cutlery and, for the most part, the family seemed full-faced and jovial.

I called to Kate and she turned abruptly. Her face flushed and she dropped the wooden spoon she had been using to stir a pot. She wiped her hands off on her apron and rushed toward us. She motioned us to go outside.

"What are you doing here? How did you find me?" she demanded.

Rarely one for small talk, Sherlock said curtly, "You are Kate Dew, daughter of the former Deputy Swan Keeper who died a few years ago."

She shook her head. "I don't know what you are talking about. Who are you?"

"I am Sherlock Holmes and I am here to find the truth."

"I don't know what you are talking about," she repeated. "Please leave."

I took Kate's hands in mine. "Kate, tell us the truth. Were you the daughter of the Queen's assistant swan keeper? Was Cecil Gray your daughter's father? Is that why you were forced to leave Her Majesty's service?"

"You need to leave me alone," she whispered but tears were starting to drip from those haunted blue eyes.

"Have you been killing Her Majesty's swans to get even?" Sherlock pressed.

"Stop it, Sherlock," I warned. I turned again to Kate. "Please, Kate. There is more to this than swans, isn't there? You do know that Cecil Gray is dead. That someone killed him. You told me that you were assaulted because you saw something you shouldn't. What did you see, Kate? Did you witness his demise?"

Sherlock piped up again. "You are in very serious trouble, Miss Dew, if you have slaughtered Her Majesty's swans."

"Sherlock!" I protested.

"But," he added quickly, "We can protect you from that. You must tell us what you saw."

She paced back and forth, wringing her hands and crying.

"The authorities will take away your daughter, Miss Dew," Sherlock said.

"The authorities! My daughter will be killed if I say anything to anyone!"

I put my hand on her shoulders. "Kate, please. It's time to tell the truth."

Kate bid her friends good night and walked with us toward her lodgings but said not another word. Finally, just before we got to where she lived, she said, "All right. But you must promise me this. My daughter Mary will be taken care of, no matter what happens. Will you swear this to me? Dr. Stamford, if you swear, I shall believe you."

Before I could respond, Sherlock intervened. "I promise you that nothing will happen to you or your daughter."

She leaned against the brick wall next to the door and slid down until she collapsed on the pavement. I bent over. "Kate, please."

Between sobs, she choked out the entire story.

21

"What I told you about my father—that was all true. He was a Deputy Keeper of the Swans. Then he became ill. His heart, it was. And he injured his leg as well. Mum died when I was little and he was always worried about me. About what would become of me if something happened to him. That's why he brought me to work with him, trained me to take his place. But it had to appear to everyone that I was a male. Ironic, isn't it? Her Majesty, the most important person in the country, is a woman and yet a lowly swan keeper cannot be a woman."

Sherlock said, "But the Queen is only in her position because there was no male heir. She is the daughter of Prince Edward, Duke of Kent, the fourth son of King George III and both the Duke and the King died. When her father's three brothers also died, leaving no surviving legitimate children, she was the only one left. So it—"

"Sherlock!" I shouted. "Stop it."

He could be so confounding and in many ways, misogynistic. And usually at the least appropriate times. It was always exasperating.

"Go on, Kate," I urged.

Kate tilted her head and, with the cuff of her blouse, wiped away tears that streamed down her cheek. "I continued on after Papa stopped tending to the swans," she said. "I'd learned so much from him. I knew everything about the swans. And the head keeper is something of a dolt. Most of them are, in fact. Abnett, now he's a good lad, but too young to supervise."

"The name is familiar to me."

130

"It is?"

"I spoke with him. He knew of no one who wished to harm Her Majesty's swans. Except you, of course. "

"Oh," she sighed and looked away. "Often Cecil—Sir Gray would come to visit the swans in the pond and just walk," she went on. "He always looked forlorn. Sad. We would talk sometimes and somehow . . . I don't know how it happened really . . . we became . . . close. We used to go to The Charring Cross or sometimes the Craven Family Hotel, down on Craven Street. He knew the proprietor. He would talk to me for hours. Sometime he would take me to Simpson's for a meal.

"He had a daughter, a little girl about eight years old," she whispered. "Her name was Alexandrina, named for the queen . . . for her real name, I mean. But she was, he said, a very strange child. She had fits and would fly into a rage and couldn't seem to learn to speak or write. They tried to teach her at home but nothing would work. She would slam cupboards and pound her head against things. She had become quite violent, often beating her mother and attacking her father or anyone who came calling. Cecil—Sir Gray—was beside himself. He contacted an acquaintance. A professor at Oxford."

"Danford Hopgood?" Sherlock asked.

Kate nodded. "Cecil told me that Hopgood studies the brain. Heads. How people's faces are shaped and the like."

"What else did he tell you? Sir Gray . . . did he hope to gain some understanding of his daughter's malady then?"

Sherlock asked. "And please be precise in the details, Miss Dew."

"I shall make myself plain. He told me that he was financing this professor's research. He'd been for years."

"Wait," Sherlock said. "He confided all of this to you? But why would he tell you all—"

Dear heavens, Sherlock could be daft! Obviously, Cecil felt he could tell Kate things that he could not share with his wife or anyone else. "Sherlock," I cried. "Stop interrupting the poor girl."

He looked perplexed but said, "Yes, of course. I am all attention. Pray, go on with your narrative."

Kate turned to me then. "When he found out I was with child, he sent me away. As I told you, he couldn't chance a scandal. He assured me that he was sending me to a safe place. He sent me to a woman in Knightsbridge who ran several brothels. She treated me well at first, but when the baby was born, she tossed us both out, so I found work on the streets. I had to support myself and I had to take care of Mary."

"How does this research work, Kate?" Sherlock asked. "Where does Hopgood get his specimens?"

"The poor. The cast out. Corpses that were sent to Oxford on the dead trains. He'd take the heads and—" Her voice trailed off. "But Cecil also financed him further.

"Then, not long ago, just a few weeks ago, Cecil sent word to me. He asked me to meet him. I don't know why I did," she admitted.

But I knew. When you loved someone completely, you could find yourself acting in total discord to the very essence of your soul.

"I met him once at the ladies' entrance to the Turkish Bath . . . at Neville's. We met again at the Doulton Pottery factory at Lambeth High. Do you know of it?"

"Yes, I know of it," Sherlock said. "They used to make drainpipes and such but now they make stoneware there."

I nodded. My Aunt Susan had many pieces of Doultonware and the privy on the first floor of Uncle's home was decorated with Lambeth Faience from the factory. "It's near the Thames," I said.

She said, "Yes. He bought me a pretty cup and saucer and then we walked along the Thames that evening. He told me that Hopgood's research had done nothing. He was no closer to knowing how to improve his daughter's lot than he'd been before and he intended to stop funding the research. And he also told me that his daughter was very ill. He wanted to know if he could take my Mary. Raise her as his own daughter. Which she is, of course. I would have none of it. If I have to lay on my back until I take my dying breath to keep my girl and feed her, then I'll do it," she added defiantly.

"A few nights ago, he sent word to me to meet him at St. Marylebone Cemetery. And that's when I found out his little girl had died. Died from the relentless fog. And he begged me again to let him raise Mary. He promised me I'd be taken care of as well. We were arguing when a man came upon us. He started yelling at Cecil."

133

"He had followed you?"

"Cecil. He'd followed Cecil. Apparently he had told the professor that he was done with him. There'd be no more money. His child was dead and he was done with all of it. He was about to go to the police about Hopgood's illegal grave robbing activities, even if it cost him his position. He didn't care anymore.

"The man at the grave became enraged. He grabbed a shovel from nearby. There have been many new graves dug there recently. He hit Cecil across his back and then the back of his head.

"I started to run. I ran as fast as I could. But he hit me, too. Many times. He was going to kill me I think, but we heard voices and I scrambled to my feet and ran until I couldn't run anymore."

I drew in a breath. "So, Sherlock. What do you think?"

He propped his hands beneath his chin as if in prayer. "I believe he killed Sir Gray. And when it was safe, he drew instruments he'd carried with him and dismembered him and tossed him into the child's grave."

I felt as though I were going to vomit.

"Kate, you were injured again—after that first time I saw you. There was a large welt on your cheek and a cut above your left eye. Did Hopgood do that?"

"Yes. He found me. I don't know how, but I've thought about that. I had a late . . . appointment . . . ." She almost choked on the word. "An appointment and I was still wearing my costume beneath my coat. I tripped over my coat as I ran. So when I stopped to catch my breath beneath a street lamp, I cast off my coat and then I started to run again. He—"

"He could have seen your sleeves. They look like wings," I interrupted. "And if he knew Cecil had a mistress—a woman who . . . who does what you do . . . he could have found your description in the *Bachelor's Pocket Book*."

"The what?" Sherlock asked.

"Never mind. Go on, Kate," I urged.

"All I know is he found me and when he did, he made it clear that he'd kill my girl if I told anyone anything. And he will."

She started to cry again.

"I was so frightened," she continued. "I was afraid to go to the authorities. But . . . but . . . ."

"Yes, yes, go on," Sherlock urged.

"I went to where Cecil told me he would take money to arrange the grave robbing for Hopgood. I knew the pub owner. We all know one another round here."

"And?" Sherlock queried, leaning forward.

"And I paid to have Cecil's daughter's grave unearthed. You see, that night I met Cecil there, when the man—Hopgood—attacked us . . . I just knew he'd killed Cecil. I went back just before dawn. The flowers Cecil had brought were tossed aside, strewn about. And the dirt had been overturned. So I wanted to make sure that someone discovered Cecil . . . Cecil's body. That's why my note said to await further instructions at the gravesite. That way Cecil wouldn't be put on a dead train and—"

"And you gave no thought to what might happen to young Wiggins!" Sherlock shouted angrily.

She shook her head. "I didn't think of anything except poor Cecil."

Realizing the predicament that Kate had put him in, Wiggins lunged for her, but Sherlock tripped him and he went sprawling on the cobblestone. He sprang back up quickly but Sherlock pushed him against the wall. Forefinger to Wiggins' nose, he said, "No. Not now."

Wiggins shrugged him away and crossed his arms.

"I'm sorry," Kate said. "I just wanted Cecil to be found. That's all. And I hoped the police would be able to sort things out without me telling anyone anything."

"Alright," Sherlock sighed. "I see." He paused but a fraction of a second and asked, "Now about the swans, Kate," Sherlock said. "Is it you? Have you been killing the swans?"

"Sherlock," I said, "as much as I love the swans, does that really matter right now?"

He shrugged. "Only for closure of the case, Poppy. Only to be certain I am correct."

"No!" Kate yelled. "I was angry and hurt and did not know any other life. I hated what had been done to my father. To me. But I would never hurt the swans. I loved them. I used to lie in the grass sometimes and watch them fly. Mute Swans . . . their wingbeats make a beautiful throbbing sound when they fly." Her face softened as she said this, almost as if she could hear them and this imaginary sound calmed her. "And they loved me," she added. "I could feed them right out of my hand."

Incredulous, Sherlock looked at me and then back at Kate. Her face flushed deep red. "I was so angry. I was forced into this. Forced into this life even though I was the best assistant swan keeper Her Majesty could have wanted. I was forced to leave before it became apparent that I was with child . . . and why? Why does it have to be that way?"

I had asked myself that many times. I had fought hard to become a physician, yet I was not fully accepted as such. I could never be a surgeon at St. Bart's. I could never be a member of the College of Royal Surgeons who don't admit women. No matter how bright or educated, there would always be doors which were closed to me.

I touched Kate's shoulder. "You're telling us the truth? You did not hurt the swans?"

She shook her head. "One of the males used to knock his head against my knee with his beak to get fed. I could hand feed most of them. I can't tell you the joy those swans brought me, watching them. Oh, and the babies. And then my hands were empty and I just wanted to cry all the time. I would never hurt them. I swear this to you."

"Then who?" Sherlock asked. "Who is doing this?"

"I tell you I don't know."

"We must get to the bottom of this, Poppy. But as to the murder of Cecil Gray matter . . . Miss Dew, you have no idea where Hopgood is, do you?"

She shook her head. "But I did hear Cecil say once that out of concern for being discovered, he often did his . . . his work at the home of his sister. She lives in Chippy."

Puzzled I looked at Sherlock. "Chipping Norton. It's a busy market town." He turned to Wiggins, handed him several coins, and said, "Take Miss Dew and her child to Montague Street. Do not let them out of your sight and do not touch a hair on her head. You understand? You do not leave her side."

Wiggins grimaced but nodded.

Sherlock gently touched Kate's shoulder. "We'll soon have matters right. I swear it."

22

Although I urged Sherlock to contact the authorities and let Mycroft in on what we knew, he insisted that we find Hopgood and 'solve this case ourselves.' He said, "When I go into a case, I do not present to the authorities half-proven theories or bits and pieces of evidence. I work out my own theories and play out the game until I know that I am correct. And it shall be so this time.

"But first a visit to Thomas Abnett is in order."

"Abnett, the young swan keeper?"

"The same."

"I have clearly come to a grievously erroneous conclusion as to the swan matter."

"We both were on the entirely wrong scent, Sherlock. I also thought it was Kate."

"It is most dangerous to reason with insufficient data. There must be someone who can get close enough to the swans to do them harm yet not be suspected. Someone who has a grievous need for revenge against the queen or the swans or both. I shall devote the same care to the Gray case as I have all cases but we must resolve this matter before we leave London."

"Leave London?"

He did not answer. He simply prodded me along until before long, we were knocking at the door to the cottage where Abnett, the young assistant swankeeper, lived. Sherlock woke him with his pounding and he opened the door bleary-eyed. Sherlock barged in.

"Abnett, you remember me?"

"'Course I do. You're Sherlock Holmes."

"This is my friend and associate, Dr. Stamford. We are here to inquire again about the swans who have been mutilated."

"Again?"

"Yes, again," Sherlock huffed. "Now, is there anyone here who has been employed but a short time? Two years or so?"

"Well, when Deputy Dew died and then after the Dew boy left, we needed another hand. So we did hire someone. His name is Matthew Bass."

"And what do you know of him?"

The boy shrugged. "Not much, Sir. Just that he came highly recommended. He used to tend to the swans at Bishops Palace at Wells Cathedral in Wells."

"There are swans there?"

"Absolutely. In fact, Mr. Bass said they ring the bells."

"What?" I gasped. "The church bells?"

"No, bells attached to them with string. That's how they beg for food. They ring for lunch. You see, Lord Hervey, he's the Bishop of Bath and Wells. Bass told me that one of Hervey's daughters trained the swans—the ones in the five-sided moat at the palace. She trained them to ring bells by pulling strings, to beg for food. They eat right out of the caretakers' hands."

Sherlock turned to me. "So it's just as Kate said then. They do eat out of someone's hands. Someone they trust. It would be easy then to poison them." He turned back to Abnett. "Good lad. Do you know why Mr. Bass left Wells and came here to tend to the royal swans?"

"He said something about his daughter getting hurt in the moat and he couldn't stand to be there anymore."

"I see. Where can I find this Matthew Bass?"

He gave us an address near St. Bart's in one of the lodgings where many of the medical students lived. My brother had resided in a flat there when he was in training. "He knows a doctor who lives round there," Abnett said. "He was sharing a room with him, I think."

"Good. Thank you. Good night then, Abnett."

With that, we left and I strained to keep up with Sherlock as we made our way toward Giltspur Street. The wind was howling and rain beat down so hard, it stung my face as we walked. Amid the gale, we searched and finally found the right location. Sherlock pounded on the door.

"Go away," said a man from within.

"I need to speak with Matthew Bass."

"What if he doesn't want to talk with you?"

Sherlock's eyebrows arched. "I have word of your daughter, sir."

The panel snapped open. A man in his late thirties with long, black hair and a rough beard opened it and rubbed his eyes sleepily. "What? What are you going on about?"

"Are you Matthew Bass? The swan keeper? The swan killer?"

The man's knees gave way. He pitched backward and slumped to a camp bed.

"I am Sherlock Holmes and I need to speak to you about the swans."

"Not about my daughter?"

141

"Only incidentally, sir. I understand that your daughter was injured in the moat at Wells Cathedral."

"Who told you that?"

"Irrelevant. Is it true? What happened? Was she injured in the moat? Or was she attacked by a swan?"

As if some long-repressed anger and rage could keep still no longer, he said, "First it was the dog. And then it was my sweet girl."

"I don't understand," I said quietly.

"You killed the swans for revenge, didn't you, sir?" Sherlock asked.

Suddenly, finally defeated, Bass's eyes welled up.

"The damn swans. They were always fine except at breeding time. We warned everyone to stay away then. But the dog got loose and took off and ran into the moat.

"Elton was just playing. A spaniel, he was. He was playing and jumped in the water. Provoked the cob, I guess. He and his lady lost cygnets in some kind of shooting incident earlier in the year. And them cobs, they're territorial. They attacked him, killed him. Drowned him. We told everyone not to go near them. But dogs are stupid. And some people. A couple boys were rowing one day and they were out near the nesting spot and the male was upset and it went at the boat, tipping it. I went out, waist deep, and helped the boys out of the water."

"I told you, Sherlock. They can be very defensive if they feel threatened."

"And then my little girl," Bass croaked and averted his eyes.

"Yes, yes," Sherlock said. "Go on."

142

"My little girl. She didn't know better. She addled the eggs in the nest. They were damaged and couldn't hatch. And the next time she went down by the river . . . you see, the eggs. We found them in a nearby nest and they were addled, so they couldn't hatch," he repeated. "She didn't mean it."

"What happened to your daughter?" I whispered.

"Her eyes. The animal poked out her eyes!" he cried, his eyes red now from crying. "I broke its neck. I snapped it. And they fined me! They fired me! The damn swans are more important than people."

"How did you come to be employed here, tending to the royal swans?" Sherlock asked.

"I used the name of a swankeeper who died a few years ago, before Bishop Hervey took over. My real name is Will Stockett, but they didn't ask a lot of questions. It was easy. It was all easy. I answered an advertisement and bought some thornapple. And then I . . . I . . . ." He stuttered and sputtered a moment. "I am not proud of what I did and I know I am a horrible person. I wanted to show them all. I wanted all of them dead, every swan in the empire. My girl can't see and yet the swans were more important than she was. I wanted to show them."

"You must come with me. You must—"

I touched Sherlock's arm. "A word?"

Stockett buried his head in his hands. We moved to a corner of the room. "Sherlock, can't we just let him go? His little girl is blind. It's difficult to blame him."

"But you yourself told me of the fines and penalties for—"

143

"His little girl is blind," I repeated. "Because of the swans, she's blind. Can't we let him go? Sherlock?"

Sherlock took a deep breath and turned back to Stockett. "Where is your daughter now, sir?"

"In Bristol, with my wife and her parents."

"Your freedom depends upon your compliance with what I say. It is essential now that you follow my advice in all respects."

"I don't understand, Mr. Holmes. I—"

"I believe that the Somerset & Dorset Joint Railway now has service to Bristol, sir. I suggest that you get on the next train to join your family."

"What?"

"I will be round again in 48 hours. Do not be here, sir."

We left quickly and were once again standing in the cold with the fog swirling at our feet. Sherlock put his hands on my shoulders and asked, "So, Poppy, are you up for a trip to the Cotswolds to solve our next case?"

23

Within hours, and after a terrible argument about it with Uncle, we were off to Chippy.

We took the train to Oxford. Then we transferred to the Chipping Norton Railway, which carried us to the depot that linked the town with Kingham via the Oxford, Worcester and Wolverhampton Railway. Sherlock and I both felt the tedium of travel, but we also highly anticipated what we would discover upon our arrival.

As the train pulled into town at nightfall, Sherlock turned to me and said, "Did you know that Sarah Averell Wildes was born here?"

"Who?"

"One of the Salem witches. She was wrongfully convicted, of course, and executed by hanging, though she maintained her innocence and was later exonerated. Her husband's first wife was one of the primary accusers. Another good example of why not to marry."

I looked out the window and sighed. Sherlock cared little for trivia, but if it helped him prove a point, he would always manage to find a way to sneak in some minutia from his brain attic to do so.

We found our way to an inn and then set out for a meal, though Sherlock did not wish to eat. He wanted to find Elizabeth Jane Hopgood, the murderer's sister. But I coaxed him into finding a place to eat by telling him he might be able to get information from the locals. We ended up at the Fox, an ancient stone-built pub near the marketplace. We ordered chipped beef and some ale, but Sherlock immediately began asking people about the

145

Hopgoods. I had barely eaten a mouthful when he yanked at my arm as he downed his ale, saying, "The sister lives on a hilltop in Stow-on-the-Wold, not far from here. We can rent a carriage just down the road from here. Let's go."

It was pitch dark and oppressive as we approached the house to which Sherlock had been directed. It was bramble-covered and ominous, but caught up in the adrenalin of the adventure, London seemed dull and distant.

Sherlock knocked on the door and almost immediately a tall, heavily built woman opened it. Her black mane was sprinkled with grey and she wore thick glasses.

When Sherlock introduced himself and said he was looking for Danford Hopgood, she tried to slam the door in our faces, but Sherlock elbowed his way in. "Where is your brother?" he demanded.

"Why do you ask about him?"

"Because he is suspected of murder."

"He is no murderer. I'll be damned if I tell you anything!" she screamed.

Sherlock stepped toward her. "Your brother is a mad man."

"My brother is a brilliant scientist. He will determine how a murderer's brain works! Just like Lombroso! You don't know anything. None of you do."

Unaccustomed to being spoken to by a woman in such a fashion—with the possible exception of myself—

Sherlock whirled around, placed his hands on her neck, choking her and pushing her up against a wall. Very deliberately he said, "Where is he?"

For a moment, she stared at him in complete silence. He shoved her away. Then he glanced around the entry and pulled her toward the kitchen. He yanked a lacy curtain from the window, tore off a slim fragment, and tossed it to me. "Bind her feet," he said as he took another remnant and bound her hands behind her back.

"Sherlock, are you sure we should—?"

He gave me a stern look, so I protested no further. I followed his instructions and then we began searching through the house. Soon he made his way to the door at the top of the stairs that led to the summer kitchen in the cellar.

He opened it, peered into the darkness and glanced at me. I nodded and followed him down the steps.

24

I touched Sherlock's shoulder. "She mentioned Lombroso, Sherlock, as you did before." I whispered. "Is it his work that Hopgood is following then?"

"Lombroso is an Italian surgeon. A few years ago, he conducted a postmortem on a serial murderer and rapist. He discovered a hollow part of the killer's brain, and he proposed that violent criminals were throwbacks to less evolved human types, identifiable by ape-like physical characteristics."

Sherlock fumbled in the darkness and finally found lanterns and lit several. What we saw when the cellar was illuminated was the most grotesque and frightening display I'd ever witnessed.

On table after table were severed heads. Torsos were tossed in baskets in a corner. Some heads were shaved with markings on them indicating different sections of the brain and the so-called correlating behaviors.

This caught me off-guard in a way that even emergency medical situations had not and I felt myself wobble. Sherlock seized my arm and steered me back toward the stairs. I sat down on the bottom step. As he walked from table to table, he said, "It really began in Italy in 1871 when Lombroso met with a criminal, a man named Giuseppe Villella, a notorious thief and arsonist. Cesare Lombroso is an army doctor, who worked in lunatic asylums and become interested in crime and criminals while studying Italian soldiers. He wanted to pinpoint the differences between lunatics, criminals and normal individuals by examining inmates in Italian prisons.

"Lombroso found Villella interesting," Sherlock continued, seemingly unaffected by the hideous and gruesome evidence before him. "So, when Villella died, Lombroso conducted a post-mortem and discovered that his subject had an indentation at the back of his skull, which resembled that found in apes. Lombroso concluded that some people are born with a propensity toward crime and were also savage throwbacks to early man."

Sherlock wandered over to a bookcase along the stone wall. He took a book from the shelf, tapped it and walked over to hand it to me. "Lombroso wrote this," he said. "*The Criminal Man*, published just a few years ago. His interest in forensics and crime is interesting but a bit warped. He seems to think that by looking at a skull, by considering palm lines and the size of orbits and cheek bones and so on, one can determine if the person is like an ape, if he's insensitive to pain, if he craves evil for evil's sake. Essentially, Lombroso believes that criminality is inherited and that criminals can be identified by physical defects that show them to be savage-like."

Staring down at the skull of what appeared to be a youth, Sherlock said, "According to Lombroso," he said, "a thief can be identified by his expressive face and small, wandering eyes. Murderers have cold, glassy stares, bloodshot eyes and big hawk-like noses." He touched his nose and said, "I shudder to think how he would think of me.

"And rapists have what Lombroso calls 'jug ears'. He also says that female criminals are more ruthless than males and that they are shorter and wrinkled and have

149

darker hair and smaller skulls than normal women. And ones with prominent lower jaws are supposedly more wicked than all of the men put together. In my opinion, it's madness."

"Sherlock, this is . . . words fail me. We must find this monster. He is the one whose skull should be studied."

"I concur."

25

Sherlock extinguished the lanterns and we went back upstairs. Sherlock once again attempted to extract information from Hopgood's sister but she refused to speak. Had I not been there, I believe he would have resorted to tactics a bit more brutal than mere interrogation. When she started screaming, Sherlock gagged her with a dish towel.

He found a box of matches and lit a lamp. He placed that in the middle of the table. He took his revolver from beneath his coat and laid it down on a corner of the table. Then he found a bottle of port and took two glasses from the cupboard.

"What are you doing, Sherlock? Shouldn't we contact the local—?"

"We wait. I am certain he will return."

"How do you suppose he managed to dismember Sir Gray's body and place it in the coffin? I mean, the cemetery is not hidden by woods or—"

"Kate said she heard voices, which gave Hopgood pause, just long enough for her to get away. I suspect they were passersby and once he was sure that no one was about, he proceeded with his grisly task. The fog covers everything, Poppy. I would guess that he intended to kill Sir Gray all along. He came prepared to do so. Gray had cut off funds. He knew too much. That's why he followed him. Hopgood did not expect to encounter Kate and she is fortunate to have escaped him. But with Kate's help, we have arrived at the truth of it."

He tapped his fingers idly on the table and sipped his wine calmly. I was, on the other hand, extremely nervous and paced the kitchen constantly. Hopgood's sister was tied up, there were a dozen severed heads beneath me, and we had no idea how dangerous the upcoming encounter would be.

An hour passed, then two. Sherlock finally asked, "What is it? What is bothering you?"

"Bass. Or Stockett. Whatever. I'm wondering why you did not try to bring him to the authorities. And Kate. I hate to see her forced to live like this."

"As to Mr. Stockett, it was you who persuaded me to let him go. And I agree. Who would it serve? Who needs to know that he is the swan assassin?"

I wondered if he would be so generous had someone killed his bees.

"I care nothing for swans, you understand," he emphasized. "Unfortunately, Mycroft has no suspect and if no more swans are killed—" His voice trailed off as he shrugged. "Then again, he has more important things to worry about."

"But if you do not tell him you've found the culprit, are you not conceding that you could not solve the case?"

He shrugged again. "And what is bothering you about Kate?"

"I hate that she has to make a living for herself in such a way," I said.

He thought for a moment. I always thought if I listened hard enough I might hear the grinding of the wheels inside his head. "Did you not tell me that your aunt's new cook is quite abysmal?"

I nodded.

"And didn't Kate's acquaintance say that she is an excellent cook?"

He tapped on the table again and said, "Something to think about."

I thought back to how kind he had been to Mrs. Hudson even though she had been something of an accomplice in the blackmail scheme crafted by her estranged husband. Sherlock could be quite compassionate at times—if his compassion seemed logical and practical.

At one point, Sherlock looked at me, a serious expression, a pained expression on his face, and his skin almost white and grave. "Poppy," he said, "about Jonathan Younger . . . ."

"It's all right, Sherlock. Don't give it another thought."

"But this story is not over yet, Poppy. I think worse dangers than me or Dr. Younger await you. You are so very trusting."

"What?"

"You must take care to choose carefully. I am not the right man for you to marry. We both know that."

"Sherlock, I—"

"But I want you to take my advice. Be on your guard. Do not let your head be turned by the likes of Jonathan Younger. Could I but journey through time, far ahead, and know what is in store for you, I might rest more easily. But as of now, I do not know how or where your story will find its end."

Part of me was desolate. I so wanted to continue to encourage Sherlock, to share in his endeavors. Often I was like a woman hypnotized. But it grieved me to do so, to continue to fawn over him, to long for him, and I knew full well that he had forced himself to become incapable of returning my affection, if he indeed had ever been truly capable of doing so. I must control my feelings. I must move on.

I looked into his frank, misty grey eyes.

"I am convinced, Sherlock, that you care for me deeply, that you always have and that you had my best interests at heart. You were just so very abrupt about Jonathan."

"What will you do about Jonathan?"

"Do? Nothing. He means nothing to me, Sherlock. Don't you realize—?" I stopped short of sharing my deepest fantasies and longing yet again. There was no point. "I shall advise Michael of his friend's indelicate behavior. I am curious, though, as to why Jonathan pursued me at all. He should have been quite disappointed in his expectations."

His gaze met my eyes. Something sprang forth but quickly disappeared again into the darkness, the vacuum that remained where emotions may have once stirred. "Disappointed in expectations of you? Quite impossible."

"I mean simply that I would not be the kind of wife he seeks. One who is submissive, rather foggy minded. There to adore him and give him children and look the other way should his eyes and passions wander."

"There are others like him out there. You must be cautious. It would do you good to burden your memory with what you saw transpire between Jonathan and that woman. People are not to be trusted."

"Not even me. You have never really trusted me."

With a dry chuckle, he said, "Not even you? No, Poppy, of all the people I've known, you are the most trustworthy. And, as I said, one of the most trusting. Do guard your emotions."

A quarter of an hour later, we heard someone playing with the doorknob. Sherlock sprang to his feet, took up his gun and motioned for me to get out of sight. I grabbed a rolling pin that was within reach. Then he blew out the candle and we were left in darkness, waiting for the door to open. When it did, Sherlock sprang from behind the door and lifted his gun to throttle the man he thought was Hopgood.

But I struck a match and saw a shadow; it was then I knew that it could not be the skinny man that Inspector Hopkins had described."Wait! Sherlock! It's not—"

Sherlock realized at the last moment. He was staring not at Professor Hopgood but at his brother Mycroft.

"What are you doing here, Mycroft?" Sherlock shouted.

"I'm doing a dear friend a favor." He turned to me. "Your uncle, Poppy. And," he added, as he held out his hand for the rolling pin, "two weapons are better than one. As are two Holmes brothers."

I looked over Mycroft's shoulder and saw a man with a ruddy face and dark, passionless eyes. Sherlock pushed Mycroft aside and pointed his gun at the intruder's chest.

He quietly said, "Professor Hopgood, I presume."

26

Staring intensely at Hopgood, Sherlock said, "It is immensely satisfying to encounter a criminal whose wit is a challenge and whose ingenuity and innovation make him a worthy opponent. Sadly, sir, you fit neither category."

"Who are you?" Hopgood demanded, his voice hissing like a snake.

"My name is Sherlock Holmes and everything is now in order."

Hopgood blinked at us and looked as dazed as one who witnesses an explosion.

"Are you a police officer? Did someone from Oxford send you here?"

"Neither," Sherlock laughed.

I saw Hopgood glance around, clearly seeking escape, but Sherlock pounded on him and knocked him to the floor.

"Professor Hopgood, in the name of Her Majesty, I arrest you for the murder of Sir Cecil Gray. We have an eye witness."

"You said you are not a police officer," Hopgood hissed.

"Did I?"

Hopgood tried to struggle and Mycroft hovered over him with the rolling pin. "I, on the other hand," he said, a smug smile crossing his lips, "am here with Her Majesty's authority."

"I assure you, Professor Hopgood," Sherlock said, "it will go much easier for you if you do not resist."

Resist he did, and Sherlock landed several well placed blows to his face and chest. They struggled for a moment and Hopgood attempted to seize the gun but instead he received a crashing blow to his temple from its butt.

As I so often did, I stared at Sherlock in amazement. "What shall I do, Sherlock?"

"Go back to the Inn and ask them to fetch the local constable."

"Yes, run along, Dr. Stamford," Mycroft said. "The constable is expecting you."

27

That night, after the local authorities were convinced to cart off Hopgood for further questioning by Inspector Lestrade, who had accompanied Mycroft from London, Mycroft, Sherlock and I had a glass of wine at the pub. Mycroft told us that my uncle had sent a page to fetch him and that he and Lestrade had hopped the next train to Chippy.

"I have told you, brother, to stay out of Her Majesty's business. How many times must I—"

"Oh, do be quiet, Mycroft," Sherlock scoffed. "I . . . we solved the case, didn't we?"

"Once again putting yourself and this young woman in danger. But now, do tell me the details."

Sherlock explained, with great flourish, I might add, the information we'd received from Kate Dew. He made no mention whatsoever of swans. Later, he said, "I tell Mycroft only what he needs to know."

As I listened to Sherlock's account of the case to his brother Mycroft, I thought to myself that despite everything, I was lucky to know him. He had changed my life in many ways, some good, some bad, but definitely in a powerful way. He had engaged me in my life's most exciting adventures.

When Sherlock had finished, Mycroft turned to me. "Dr. Stamford, I must see what Lestrade is up to now, but I gave your uncle my word that I would see you home safely."

"There are no trains until morning, Mycroft," I said.

"Yes, yes, unfortunately. Have you arranged for lodging?"

Simultaneously, Sherlock and I replied, "We have a room."

Mycroft's eyebrows shot up. "Young lady, your uncle—"

"What I meant, what we meant, Mycroft, is that Sherlock and I already made arrangements at the inn. We have rooms. Both of us."

Again, Mycroft eyed us suspiciously but finally shrugged and said, "I'll see you in the morning then. Eight sharp." As he bid us goodnight, he said, "I shall expect a written report from you in the morning, Sherlock."

As Mycroft stepped away from the table, we both laughed and then Sherlock muttered, "In the morning, indeed." Then he said, "Now we must turn our attention to the rest of Hopgood's sordid business. Who knows who else he may have received funding from?"

"Not tonight, Sherlock. Not tonight. Can't we talk about something else?"

So then he turned his monologue to his bees. And I thought how akin he was to the bees he studied. They knew exactly what they were to do and did it in the most efficient way possible.

The iconic pattern, the hexagonal cells that form a honeycomb is well known. Like Sherlock's cases, each individual cell has a story to tell. The concise and orderly pattern of the comb is a symbol for structure, order, utility and strength and none of this is by accident. Bees long ago discovered a way to build their homes, their lives, which serves them well.

Worker bees have 8 pairs of wax glands under their abdomen, which produce small, flat scales and when a worker creates a comb, she scrapes off a wax scale from her abdomen using the spines on her pollen basket and passes them to her front legs. Holding the scale in place, she will mix it with saliva by chewing with her mandibles. This adjusts the wax, making it more suitable as a building material from which each individual cell is built. This is repeated tens of thousands of times, Sherlock told me, and they form the beehive. This establishes their home, their lives. Their choice is a simple approach, a logical approach that works well for them. It is a place to store honey and essential for them to survive the winter.

Each type of cell in the hive has a distinct purpose. Worker cells are to raise worker bees. Drone cells are larger and this is where the drones live. Queen cells are a different shape and size.

"So," Sherlock said, "there is efficiency of space and cell building and there are no gaps whatsoever. It is airtight. Compared to other shapes like triangles and squares, the hexagon creates a comb with the least amount of material and with the greatest of strength. A honeycomb of just 100 grams supports weight up to 4 kilograms."

I smiled. He had in essence described himself. Efficient, strong, shaping his life perfectly with no allowance for gaps, with no possibility for vulnerability or anything that might diminish his strength and logical progression.

Sherlock was like a bee. He knew exactly and perfectly what he must do to keep his logical life on a strict and efficient course.

We had arranged for a double-bedded room at the inn. Sherlock tossed his coat and jacket over a chair, kicked off his boots, and plopped down on the bed on the right. He slept in his trousers and shirt. I, of course, wore my dress to bed. As I lay down by myself on the other bed, just inches away from Sherlock, I stared up at the ceiling. How unseemly my mother and father would have thought of this arrangement, I thought. Yet how innocent this was compared to the time we'd shared at Home-Next-the-Sea. I had never spoken to anyone, least of all my parents, of the romantic tryst Sherlock and I had shared long ago . . . that one time that we shared and enjoyed our bodies and gave way to our true feelings. It seemed like another lifetime.

As he slept, moonlight shone through the window. I stared at him in the darkness of the room, his face peaceful now, so content he was that another case was solved. He was on the blazing threshold of an illustrious career but one I could not share with him. For him there could be no expression of emotion. No passion. Certainly no marriage. He could only be whipped into a storm, into the zeal he exhibited, by a full and complex case to solve. He entirely abandoned himself to the exclusion of everything else, his gaze always fastened upon the Game. For all the innuendo, all the mysteries and complexities we exchanged, for all the times that love passed close to us, and the declarations of it that I'd so often hastened to share with him, I was usually invisible to him, my not-so-secret love-smitten languor met by a wall of ice.

The imprint of his persistence and the craving and yearning he'd awakened in me, in my mind and in my heart, the devotion I felt for him, could never be sated.

The curtains billowed in the breeze and they oscillated to the left and right. Fastened on his face, I fell into a profound reverie, a kaleidoscope of memories of every moment we'd spent together, memories with which I would forever be burdened. I woke at dawn and tip-toed to the window. There was only sunlight, not a smidgen of fog. Finally it was lifting.

I turned and watched Sherlock sleeping for a long time. His eyelids twitched, his face relaxed, as if he were meandering through serene surroundings. His countenance illuminated for me alone at that moment the odd grace and joy that he had found in a life wherein the heart is silenced.

He smiled in his sleep, enraptured in some sort of dream about which I could only guess.

Also from MX Publishing

MX Publishing is the world's largest specialist Sherlock Holmes publisher, with over a hundred titles and fifty authors creating the latest in Sherlock Holmes fiction and non-fiction.

From traditional short stories and novels to travel guides and quiz books, MX Publishing cater for all Holmes fans.

The collection includes leading titles such as *Benedict Cumberbatch In Transition* and *The Norwood Author* which won the 2011 Howlett Award (Sherlock Holmes Book of the Year).

MX Publishing also has one of the largest communities of Holmes fans on Facebook with regular contributions from dozens of authors.

www.mxpublishing.com

Also from MX Publishing

The Conan Doyle Notes (The Hunt For Jack The Ripper)

"Holmesians have long speculated on the fact that the Ripper murders aren't mentioned in the canon, though the obvious reason is undoubtedly the correct one: even if Conan Doyle had suspected the killer's identity he'd never have considered mentioning it in the context of a fictional entertainment. Ms Madsen's novel equates his silence with that of the dog in the night-time, assuming that Conan Doyle did know who the Ripper was but chose not to say – which, of course, implies that good old stand-by, the government cover-up. It seems unlikely to me that the Ripper was anyone famous or distinguished, but fiction is not fact, and "The Conan Doyle Notes" is a gripping tale, with an intelligent, courageous and very likable protagonist in DD McGil."

The Sherlock Holmes Society of London

www.mxpublishing.com

Also from MX Publishing

Our bestselling books are our short story collections;

'Lost Stories of Sherlock Holmes' , 'The Outstanding Mysteries of Sherlock Holmes', The Papers of Sherlock Holmes Volume 1 and 2, 'Untold Adventures of Sherlock Holmes' (and the sequel 'Studies in Legacy) and 'Sherlock Holmes in Pursuit', 'The Cotswold Werewolf and Other Stories of Sherlock Holmes' – and many more……

www.mxpublishing.com

Also from MX Publishing

The Missing Authors Series

Sherlock Holmes and The Adventure of The Grinning Cat
Sherlock Holmes and The Nautilus Adventure
Sherlock Holmes and The Round Table Adventure

"Joseph Svec, III is brilliant in entwining two endearing and enduring classics of literature, blending the factual with the fantastical; the playful with the pensive; and the mischievous with the mysterious. We shall, all of us young and old, benefit with a cup of tea, a tranquil afternoon, and a copy of Sherlock Holmes, The Adventure of the Grinning Cat."
Amador County Holmes Hounds Sherlockian Society

Also from MX Publishing

When the papal apartments are burgled in 1901, Sherlock Holmes is summoned to Rome by Pope Leo XII. After learning from the pontiff that several priceless cameos that could prove compromising to the church, and perhaps determine the future of the newly unified Italy, have been stolen, Holmes is asked to recover them. In a parallel story, Michelangelo, the toast of Rome in 1501 after the unveiling of his Pieta, is commissioned by Pope Alexander VI, the last of the Borgia pontiffs, with creating the cameos that will bedevil Holmes and the papacy four centuries later. For fans of Conan Doyle's immortal detective, the game is always afoot. However, the great detective has never encountered an adversary quite like the one with whom he crosses swords in "The Vatican Cameos."

"An extravagantly imagined and beautifully written Holmes story"
  (**Lee Child**, NY Times Bestseller, Jack Reacher series)

www.ingramcontent.com/pod-product-compliance
Lightning Source LLC
Chambersburg PA
CBHW070031260626
47159CB00005B/2017